Sgian Dubh

An Adventure Story

book one

Anthony M. Martin

Published by

MELROSE BOOKS

An Imprint of Melrose Press Limited
St Thomas Place, Ely
Cambridgeshire
CB7 4GG, UK
www.melrosebooks.com

FIRST EDITION

Copyright © Anthony M. Martin 2008

The Author asserts his moral right to
be identified as the author of this work

Cover designed by Catherine McIntyre

ISBN 978-1-906050-70-2

Printed and bound in Great Britain by:
Biddles. King's Lynn. Norfolk PE30 4LS

Mixed Sources
Product group from well-managed
forests, controlled sources and
recycled wood or fiber
www.fsc.org Cert no. TT-COC-002303
© 1996 Forest Stewardship Council

PEFC
PEFC/16-33-293
PEFC - Promoting Sustainable Forest Management

This book is dedicated to
"Sasha and her family",
with thanks to all those who
have inspired me.

Prologue

AD 140

The Sahara Desert. A cold, starry night. A Bedouin encampment. Snoring bodies sleeping within. Nearby, camels chewing slowly with eyes closed huddle together. A sudden flash of light. A deafening roar. A red-hot meteor ploughs into the sand. Silence. A cloud of pungent-smelling smoke rises slowly, revealing a massive crater. The caravan is no more.

AD 700

The Scottish Highlands. Snowflakes vanish as they touch the still, black surface of the loch lying at the feet of a rampart of white mountains. A figure huddles in his plaid near the entrance to a dimly lit cave. His eyes are closed. A shadow creeps along the opposite wall. It stoops over a rectangular stone. Light from a flickering fire glistens on a burnished oval protrusion on the side of the grey block of stone. It is gripped by a hand.

Whoosh!

"Ahhhh!!!"

"Basaich!" (Die as a brute!) The clan war cry echoes around the cavern.

A claymore slices through the cold air and the intruder's arm. The hand and bleeding severed arm continue to grip the object on the side of the stone. The wounded man is dragged out into the snow. A bloody trail leads to a group of Highlanders standing by the shore.

A man with red hair, shaggy eyebrows and eyes that burn like fire is standing apart. He is dressed in a close-fitting hooded wrap. His voice is deep and threatening.

"Ronachan Maree. You dishonour your clan. Set foot on the mainland again and God's wrath will smite you and your family!"

The clan chief tears the plaid and kilt from the wounded man. He is dragged over snow-covered pebbles and thrown into the icy water. The bleeding body struggles to stay afloat for over an hour. The cold, dark water closes over his head. A sudden jolt from below. The man bursts from the loch on the slimy black back of a beast and is carried off into the night.

AD 1950

London. Christmas day. A Ford Anglia begins a long journey north. The Stone of Destiny, in two pieces, lies in the boot wrapped in a Glasgow student's overcoat.

1

*M*idnight in the rain. From time to time he saw a faint flicker of moonlight. The small, dark-haired boy crawled on hands and bleeding knees along a high, moss and lichen-covered stone wall. A two-metre gap separated the wall from an extension to the main school building.

"A wet kilt and trainers are no good for this job," he murmured.

Jumping onto a slanting, slippery roof would be interesting. It had been a dry night the first time he'd done this. The boy enjoyed climbing in the dark, despite a fear of heights in daylight. He'd never forget the day his father, in a rage, pushed him on a sledge down an icy slope.

He stood up slowly. It was like standing on ice.

"I always wondered what a ski jump would be like," he thought. "Here goes!"

He threw himself over the gap, arms and hands outstretched ready to grasp the slates.

Thump!

He slithered down, scraping fingers and knees. His feet lodged in the gutter.

"Wow! Catman would have been proud of that," the boy shouted with relief.

Sgian often identified himself with the 1940s comic character he'd discovered at a car boot sale. The boy loved cats.

He lay on the roof and looked across the wet slates shining in the moonlight.
"This is a skin job," he said, removing his socks and trainers as one.

He tied the laces together and slung the shoes round his neck. He took a black Swiss penknife with its red spotlight from his sporran, held it between his teeth and inched his way to the skylight. He knew how to release the catch from his previous exploration of the school's attic spaces. Sitting on the open window he thought about the day's events.

It had started well. Summer holidays in prospect. On his way to school he thought of how he might spend every waking hour away from home. Helping in the Botanic Garden and the market and some serious catching up on extreme sports to be done in the library.

"Hi, Alisdair!" He joined his friend in the school playground.

"How was it last night?" Alisdair asked.

"Payday night in the pub, then he explodes," replied Sgian.

His father was the skipper of a fishing boat. After days at sea he came ashore to drink and be violent. The man blamed the boy for the disappearance of his first wife, Sgian's mother. Every day, for as long as the boy could remember, his father would point an accusing finger, saying, "Why did you have to have the 'second sight'?" There was never any explanation as to what these words meant.

He and his stepmother learned the meaning of fear and pain. As a result he developed great inner strength and was a boy of few words. Raised voices kept him awake most nights. So he had turned to nocturnal activities that brought out a darker side of his character. He became skilled in climbing trees and exploring old buildings. In other words, a good cat burglar. On occasions he could not resist the temptation to 'lift' the odd small item that would sell quickly at the car boot sale.

Sgian was a daydreamer, often failing to complete his homework and rarely preparing for exams. Yet he always scraped through, to the great surprise of his teachers! It was not, as his teacher Miss MacAlister said, "Too much time at video games." The boy preferred real life to an electronic brain drain.

The last morning class was on Viking history.

"Who can tell me something about the Viking's appearance?" the teacher asked. She saw the glazed look in Sgian's eyes. A piece of chalk bounced off his desk.

"Sgian Maree Dubh, have you been listening?" The teacher loved showing off her Celtic pronunciation. It embarrassed the boy.

"Yes, Miss."

"Well, what's the answer to my question?"

"Horny helmets and bearskins, Miss," he replied with a smile. The girls giggled.

Miss MacAlistair smiled, saying, "Your colourful imagination runs away with you at times, Sgian. Here's a project for all of you during the holiday. Try to find out where the Viking's settled in Scot..." The teacher didn't manage to finish her sentence. A bell rang. There was an explosion of raised voices, the sounds of chairs and desks scraping on the floor, the thump of falling books and feet pounding towards the door.

"I'll race you to lunch, Sgi!" shouted one boy.

"You're on," was the reply.

Sgian darted between his slower, taller companions and pushed his way to the door. Suddenly he was in the dark and sounds were muffled. His momentum propelled him straight into two moving objects that gave way and separated. There was a shout followed by a deep thump. Sgian tumbled over. The waste paper bin fell from his head. He was sitting in the corridor on a sea of papers, facing the wall. He turned to confront a large, beak-like nose bearing down on him. The Headmaster was on all fours right behind him. His terrifying stare was fixed on the boy.

"Well done, boy! See me in my office after lunch. I know you! You're always in a dwam. It's discipline you need."

The Head gathered up his papers and stormed down the corridor. Pupils parted like the waters of the Red Sea as he advanced.

A loud guffaw from a tall boy. He'd lost all his hair and eyebrows after an illness and was permitted to wear a baseball cap in class.

"Mary's head's too small for a Viking helmet!" the class bully, Lachlan MacCafferty, roared.

"And it won't take much to blow yours off!" Sgian murmured.

A sudden rush of cold air through the open classroom window whisked MacCafferty's hat down the corridor. Laughter from the rest of the class.

The head gave Sgian a task to complete during the holidays. His father would be informed that he required discipline at home. Sgian feared the consequences.

'I've got to get that letter before it's posted,' he thought.

So it was that Sgian had resolved to return to his school that night and take the letter from the Head's office.

He put on his trainers, pulled the skylight closed behind him and jumped through cobwebs down to the attic floor. He walked along rafters to the hatch above the Head's office, opened it and shone his penknife torch down to the desk. He sat on the edge of the opening with the hatch door against his back. He dropped onto the desk. The hatch closed with a thump behind him.

He knew the office layout from daytime disciplinary appearances and his previous nocturnal visit. The yellow, green and brown pickled snake in a jar, the stuffed snowy owl and the school photographs were visible in the moonlight. He looked at the object hanging on the wall behind the desk. It fascinated him so much that he had never heard most of the Head's ranting. The historical map of Scotland stirred his imagination. He loved reading maps.

He searched for the letter to no avail.

"The Head must have made a copy. At least I can see what he's written," the boy mumbled.

There was a tall, green filing cabinet in one corner of the room. He dragged the Head's chair over to the cabinet and stood on it to look through the files.

"Pupil Reports. It'll be in here."

There was no sign of the letter in his file, but something else caught his eye. An entry, made on the day he arrived at the school, said, "English poor. First language Gaelic."

A vague memory was stirred.

A stair creaked. No time to replace the file. He closed the cabinet, returned the chair to the desk and crawled underneath.

"Squeak, squeak."

His hand squashed something warm and furry that had also taken refuge under the desk. The mouse scurried across the moonlit floor.

There was a fluttering outside the window and the office darkened. The office door opened. A torch was switched on. Sgian started to take slow, deep breaths in preparation for escape. He had a strange feeling he'd been in this situation before.

Ten years earlier

The whitewashed croft house faced a choppy sea loch. A solitary stunted birch tree was the only plant to survive wind, peat and rabbits. A few plants flourished round an ancient cairn on a hill behind the house. It had been used as a beacon to guide boats to safety. A fire lit within the cairn caused limestone rocks to glow. Sgian's mother called it her rockery garden.

A sunny morning. An onshore breeze blew the smell of seaweed to the boy's bedroom. Sgian lay half awake and Purdie, his tabby kitten, snuggled close by. She was the sole survivor of a wildcat litter. Mother and siblings were all killed in an avalanche. He heard the voices of his mother and father in the kitchen.

"I'll be glad when he starts school, Roddy. His mind's so active. He needs to learn English. He's desperate to read these books you brought from Inverness."

"Aye, you're right, Mairi. And then there's the other thing. How will he cope with it? The only one in a generation." His father's tone was sombre.

"Don't worry, Roddy; he'll use the gift wisely," replied his mother.

"It's a terrible responsibility," he said with a sigh. "We both know the stories of children being taken. There's someone with evil intent out there. Though for the life of me, I don't understand it. I fear for you both when I'm at the fishing."

The boy heard these words.

"Sgian, porridge is ready," his mother shouted up the stairs.

After breakfast the boy said he was going to play football with his friend Davie.

"Mind and stay away from the quick bog, Sgian," said his mother as he was leaving.

The sky was blue and cloudless. A mild breeze kept the midgies away. Sheep wandered here and there nibbling the short grass, which grew in patches on sandy banks.

"I'm goin' to be a goalie when I grow up," shouted Davie after a brilliant save.

"I'm just looking forward to wearing shoes when we start school," Sgian said after stubbing his bare feet on a rock.

"There's no' enough boys to make a team," said Davie.

"My dad said girls play football too," shouted Sgian as he ran after the returning ball. It landed near a dark rock pool. He bent down to pick it up. An image of thunderclouds flashed across the surface of the pool. He looked back towards Davie and shouted, "We'd better pack it in. It's going to rain."

His friend laughed, pointing up to the clear blue sky, and called, "You've got to be joking. Just because I'm winning."

Sgian looked up. His brow wrinkled. He shouted back, "OK, let's see how good you are."

Within five minutes Sgian had scored a goal and a sudden gust of wind blew grey-black clouds from nowhere. There was a distant rumble of thunder. Then the heavens opened.

"How did you do that, Sgi?" Davie shouted above the downpour. He didn't wait for an answer but ran home.

Sgian was soaking when he reached the little white cottage. The smell of fresh baking greeted him at the door.

"Get changed into some dry clothes, son. Pancakes and blaeberry jam are waiting for you," said his mother.

He had just finished dressing when he heard a shout from his father. There was urgency in his voice. Sgian had an uneasy feeling. As he ran downstairs, followed by Purdie, there was a flash of lightning and thunder rumbled out at sea. His father was standing at the foot of the stairs holding open a loose wooden panel under the staircase.

"Hide in here and don't make a sound, Sgian," he said.

"What's happening, Dad? I'm not frightened of thunder and lightning."

"It's something else, son. We'll tell you about it later. Whatever happens, stay quiet till I let you out." With these words he helped the boy squeeze under the stairs, then replaced the panel.

Sgian crouched down in the dark, closed his eyes and listened. For a moment the image of the dark rock pool came to him.

Some minutes later he heard the front door burst open and a deep voice boomed, "Where's the boy?"

"Who are you?" asked his father. Purdie hissed.

"He's out fishing by the loch with a friend," said his mother.

"Why don't I believe you?" was the reply.

Sgian opened his eyes. There was a tiny chink of light between two steps. He peeped through. A dark, hooded figure towered over his parents. A smell of singed hair and musty air drifted through the gap.

"You wouldn't be hiding him somewhere, would you? He has something that belongs to me," said the figure.

"How could a boy that's not yet four years old have something of yours?" said his father.

"You know he was born with it. If you don't bring him to me you'll never see your wife again. And eventually I'll have what is mine!"

There was an angry roar, a screech, a scuffle and the sound of a body falling. Sgian couldn't see or understand what happened next. The boy was terrified. He heard a cry from his mother then all was silent. Sgian broke out from his hiding place. His father lay unconscious. There was smoke in the room. His mother was gone. Purdie was gone. Sgian cried out. He opened the door and windows and saw that his father was coming round.

From that day the boy's father was a different man. He resented his son. Sgian knew he had to find out what had happened to his mother and what the 'second sight' meant. And one day he would look after another kitten.

—————◆—————

Sgian jumped at the sound of the filing cabinet drawer being pulled open.

"He's somewhere in here." The voice made the hair on the back of Sgian's neck stand on end.

Footsteps approached the wall in front of the Headmaster's desk. They stopped as if examining something. Then he recognised the musty, burning smell. Footsteps walked towards the window. It was opened. There was a fluttering sound. The window was closed. The footsteps returned to the door. The torchlight was switched off. The door closed. Creaking floorboards faded.

"Flaming firewalls. What was that all about?" The boy let out a long, slow breath. "I'm out of here!"

He crawled out from his hiding place and went to replace his personal file. The drawer was open and the files belonging to his entire year were gone!

"But what'll I do with mine? Knowing my luck, the Head'll blame everything on me when he finds them all missing."

Then the smell of smoke hit him. He dropped his file, opened the door and saw a cloud of bluish smoke wafting its way up the staircase.

"That weirdo's started a fire." He rushed to the window and opened it. He looked down from the Head's second storey office.

"It'll have to be a drainpipe job." He was about to climb out then stopped. "I'll call 999."

He dialled, ignored the operator's questions and shouted, "The Edinburgh School's on fire!" He hung up and climbed out of the window. The boy was some way along the road on his skateboard when he heard the fire engine arrive.

Two pairs of eyes, watching the school, saw the boy.

2

He was so preoccupied with the events in the Head's office that he didn't notice where his skateboard had taken him. It was 1 a.m. Still raining. Few people about. He was at the quayside. A fishing boat was tied up alongside. A door opened. Two figures emerged from a dimly lit passage. A man and woman stepped on to the quay. A taxi arrived. The couple kissed. Sgian heard the man say, "Give me a call before we sail, Liz."

The woman turned and Sgian saw his stepmother get into the car. As it drove off Sgian heard a muffled cry from steps leading down to the rising tide. He saw a cardboard box partly immersed and moving. He climbed down and opened the box. A wet and bedraggled grey cat jumped into his arms, purring and shivering.

"You're safe now," he said softly into her ear.

"What are you doing with that moggie, lad?" said a gruff voice. It was the man he'd seen kissing his stepmother. Stocky build, crew cut, coarse features. A tough-looking character. He reached for the cat, but in a flash it was gone.

"I found it down there, mister," said Sgian, pointing to the submerged box.

"That bloody cook. I gave him the sack. Good on ye, lad. You're out late? Watch your step," said the man. He turned and walked back to the quayside. Sgian saw the name *Highland Warrior*, his father's boat.

3

He lay awake for the few hours left. Dark clouds hung over his summer holidays.

'I wish I was somewhere far away,' he thought, jumping out of bed at first light. The rain had stopped. The sky was brightening. He packed a few things in his school sack.

'I'll stay away until he goes back to sea.' He'd go round to Alisdair's.

The note he scribbled for his stepmother said, 'Gone camping for a few days with Alisdair. Yours aye, S.'

Sgian slipped out the back door. He wasn't heard above the snoring coming from his father's bedroom.

He arrived at the Botanic Garden on his 'wheels', a home-made skateboard that was at least one and a half times larger than any other he had seen. A man, wearing a yellow and black tartan deerstalker hat, wobbled his way towards the west gate on his 'bone shaker', as he liked to call his old bicycle. MacKenzie was a white-haired, bearded West Highlander who'd been employed as a gardener for longer than anyone could remember.

"You're bright and early, Sgian. Been setting fire to your school have you?"

The boy's heart missed a beat and his mouth dropped open.

"Just joking. You probably haven't heard. It said on the news this morning that someone set fire to the school then called the fire brigade. Apparently, all they found was a smoke-filled room but no fire."

Sgian, looking perplexed, let out a long breath, then said, "Pity it hadn't happened yesterday morning, then maybe I wouldn't have floored the Head."

9

MacKenzie looked surprised and asked what happened. The boy told him.

"So, you need to find out where your tartan and the clan came from? I always wondered myself. I've never seen that tartan before. What do your folks say?"

"They don't have a clue and aren't interested." Sgian never told anyone what had happened to his mother. "I'll have a look at some books in the library," he added.

As they approached the greenhouse where the gardener looked after alpine plants he said, "I've just had an idea. I'm going back home for a few days. How'd you like to come to Wester Ross? Mother would love to meet you. I've often spoken about you. And Sasha would love to show you around our croft. The retired Gaelic teacher in Mellon Udrigle knows a lot about the clans. We'll pay her a visit."

"Brill!" said the boy excitedly. He thought the dark clouds might just be clearing. But they were being observed from a branch above and listened to from a shrub nearby.

"Let your folks know. The Flying Scotsman leaves from platform 19 at midday. I'll get the tickets."

After watering some plants they agreed to meet on the platform. Sgian threw his skateboard into the air and boarded it as it hit the ground running. MacKenzie couldn't see him for dust! But there was no way he was going to ask his parents!

He sped round to Alisdair's house and met him returning from his paper round.

"Hi, Sgi! Hear about the fire and Watty?"

"Watty?"

"The police came to our house this morning. He's missing. They think he may have drowned surfing down at the coast."

"What? He's the school's best swimmer!"

"No sign of him or his board. And another thing. Firemen found our reports in the grounds of the school covered in bird shit, and Watty's was missing!"

Sgi's mind was racing. 'That character in the Head's office must have been after Watty,' he thought. Then he remembered why he wanted to see Ali.

"Ali! Can you cover for me? I've told my mum I'm going camping with you. But MacKenzie at the Botanic's taking me to his croft in the Highlands. He knows people who'll help with the stuff for the Head."

"Cool! Your uncle going too?"

Sgian looked puzzled. "What uncle?"

"The guy who called my mobi this morning."

"I don't have an uncle."

"Well, whoever he was asked where he'd find you this morning. Come to think of it, how'd he get my number?" Alisdair was lost in thought for a moment then said, "He sounded a bit weird."

"What did you tell him?" asked Sgian.

"I said you'd be at the Botanic greenhouses," replied Alisdair.

Now it was Sgian's turn to pause for thought. 'Two weirdos in one day looking for something or someone.' His red alert button had just been pushed! Sgian nodded. He had the feeling he'd have to watch his back.

"I'm off then. Watch out for yourself, Ali!"

He reached the station well before time. It was a hive of activity.

"Wow! A circus without a ring," he said to no one in particular.

Every colour and style, overdressed and underdressed. No one paying the least bit of attention to anyone else. Strange words from passersby mingled with echoing, incomprehensible loudspeaker announcements and the sounds of taxis and trains. Two men stopped just beside him and started chattering in a strange language while looking at a map. Sgian heard the words 'Stone of Destiny' and then he froze!

Coming towards him was the last person he expected or wished to meet. The Headmaster! And he was accompanied by two police officers. They hadn't spotted the boy so he quickly turned to talk to the two men looking at the map.

"Can I help you?" he asked.

"Thank you, young man. We are heading for the Highlands. So far, we are not lost, but maybe your help will be needed should we meet again." They smiled and one of them shook the boy's hand. By this time the Head and his escorts had passed by and Sgian saw them heading in the direction of platform 19.

"They're looking for me! The Head must have spoken to Ali," he said to himself. "How am I going to get on the train? I must catch MacKenzie before he goes to the platform." His gaze was following the two men he'd just spoken to as they walked into a tourists' tartan shop. When he saw who was standing in the doorway an idea came to him.

No one noticed the boy leaving the shop accompanied by a tall, tartan-clad young woman. A tour bus drew up close to platform 19 and its occupants emerged.

"Perfect cover for us, Cindy," said the boy.

They moved with the crowd towards the platform. He spotted the policemen and the Head scrutinising faces on the platform.

"This'll do us nicely, Cindy," he said as they both dodged behind a pillar.

The Flying Scotsman rumbled in snorting blue diesel smoke. The waiting travellers surged forwards as the train stopped. Carriage doors opened and the passengers descended. The stationmaster, a guard and a ticket collector stood chatting. A change of catering staff and food trolleys arrived. Porters pushed loads of cases. Cyclists hunted for somewhere to store their cycles and visitors waited to welcome arrivals. The noisy crowd made the police hunt difficult. It was the right time for Cindy's finest performance.

"Now, do your stuff, Cindy," the boy said as he pushed his skateboard from behind the pillar.

She rushed forwards towards the edge of the platform and the boy yanked a string, shouting, "Help," from his hiding place. She catapulted onto the track in front of the engine. Several pairs of eyes turned to see the tartan-clad figure flying through the air. One observer shouted, pointing and running down the platform, "Someone's fallen on the track!"

Several people, including the policemen, rushed to Cindy's rescue. MacKenzie arrived just in time to witness this drama. He felt a tug at his sleeve and Sgian's voice said, "Hi, MacKenzie. Don't worry about her. Let's get our seats."

The gardener looked puzzled but just followed the boy to a carriage door. They caught sight of a policeman climbing back onto the platform with a horizontal Cindy, minus her wig and kilt, under one arm.

They found window seats. As Sgian stowed his skateboard above, MacKenzie said with a grin, "I hope that board floats. Water's the only thing that's flat on the west coast."

"I can make it roll, fly and swim anywhere," the boy replied, returning the smile.

They heard two men talking as they passed by down the carriage.

"Throwing that mannequin on the line was a publicity stunt for the tartan shop," said one.

"The mini kilt helped it fly off the walkway," added the other.

On the platform the stationmaster held his whistle at the ready, one or two well-wishers were waving goodbye and the Head with his police escort stood looking up and down the train. At the last minute a hooded figure rushed past their coach carrying a large box with air holes in it.

Sgian took out his drawing pad. MacKenzie opened his shoulder bag and brought out packs of sandwiches, crisps and bananas.

"Let me buy the drinks from the trolley," said Sgian. He'd 'borrowed' cash from his mother's purse.

The refreshed, replenished Flying Scotsman left Edinburgh and sped north. As the boy sketched the outline of the monk, the conversation he overheard came to mind.

"What's so special about the Stone of Destiny?" he asked.

MacKenzie's eyes widened with surprise for a moment.

"Strange you should ask me about that, Sgian. They say it has spiritual properties. It was brought from Egypt to Scotland by missionaries a long time ago. The Kings of Scotland were crowned sitting on it."

"A cold seat for short kilts," said the boy.

"Well, they must have liked the feel of it, the way it's been worn down by royal rears!" said MacKenzie laughing.

Sgian wondered at MacKenzie's surprise but said no more.

4

Squeaking wheels and the chink of bottles announced the arrival of the snack trolley.

"Anything from the trolley, gentlemen?" the young carriage attendant asked. Sgian was jolted out of his daydream and looked round.

"Yes, thanks. MacKenzie, what d'you fancy?"

"What's that? Oh... mmmm... yes." He was awakened from a snooze.

"A tea for me, Sgian, thanks," he replied.

"And I'll have water, please," said the boy. The young woman poured out the drinks.

Sgian emptied out the contents of his sporran. Torch, penknife, magnifying glass, two pieces of white chalk (with the 'compliments' of his teacher), toothbrush and toothpaste, a tangle of cord and coins, which he extracted and handed over.

"Looks like you're off on an expedition, young man. But where's your brolly?" she said, pointing out of the window at the heavy downpour. "Have a good time, anyway." She thanked him and trundled her trolley to the table across the passageway.

A tall, completely bald, ruddy-faced man with grey-green eyes, a huge bulbous nose and a bushy black moustache stood up to inspect the snacks. Sgian was fascinated by his long, slim fingers. The man seemed intent on buying everything on the trolley. Seeing the boy's look of amazement he said, with an American accent, "I'm off to the Scots Wild West. I reckon there won't be many eatin' places there."

The boy spotted a tall white hat on top of a red suitcase on the luggage rack. The rack, the floor and the seats opposite were stacked with travel bags. The American saw the direction of the boy's gaze.

"That's my Stetson. Keeps sun, rain and mosquitos off my shiny top," he said with a laugh, slapping his head. "Oliver Jeffrey from Colorado at your service! The kilt tells me you're from around here."

"I'm MacKenzie. This is Sgian. Where would you be heading for?" MacKenzie asked.

"I like solving mysteries and I'm hoping to catch a sight of Nessie. What d'ya think my chances are?"

"Well, the Highlands are full of mystery," MacKenzie said with a faint smile.

"I reckon it's a giant sea snake," said the American.

MacKenzie frowned, saying, "The only snake you've to be wary of in Scotland's the adder. I've been bitten once. Once more and I'll breathe my last. Watch your step among the rocks if you're climbing in the mountains."

"There ain't no chance of that. High places don't agree with me. I stick to boats. I've chartered a fishing boat to take me up the west coast."

Sgian smiled to himself, wondering if the man had ever tried heights at night.

"Sgian and I are heading to the north west. If you're near Poolewe, drop in for a cup of tea. There are one or two mysteries nearby you might be interested in. Gruinard Island's famous. No one really knows what went on there. Something to do with germ warfare in the 1940s. There's a religious sect there now. Then there's a rocky mountain that sticks out of the sea. Legend has it that you'll fall to the centre of the earth if you ever reach the summit. No one dare go there."

"What's it called?" asked the American.

"Nan Ron Slapach. The Isle of splashing seals," replied MacKenzie.

"So what's the problem? Send a chopper with some mountaineers to have a look."

"It's been tried. Every time they approach, a thick fog envelops them. The same thing happens when boats approach. Even fishermen won't go near."

"That sounds interesting. Say, how about us making an expedition together?"

This sounded like a great adventure to Sgian.

The Highlander looked thoughtful for a moment or two then spoke. "I might just take you up on that. There's something I saw that makes me think all is not as it seems on that island and I'd thought of taking a trip with the coastguards."

"What did you see?" asked the boy.

"I once saw a group of seals follow a light that disappeared into the side of the cliff," said MacKenzie.

The American's eyes narrowed. "Any other mystery up there?" he asked.

"There's the 'Inverewe Birch' in the Trust garden. It's the only evergreen birch tree. I planted it when I was an apprentice there in the 50s. And the story of the broken Stone of Destiny. I was there when the students brought it north," said MacKenzie.

"Sounds interesting and you'll be the guide, Mr MacKenzie. What's your number?" said the American.

The Highlander dug deep into his outsized Harris Tweed jacket. He produced the biggest mobile Sgian had ever seen. The American's eyes widened.

"Now there's something. You must have one of the original cellphones from way back."

"Well, it might be at that. I picked it up at a car boot sale. It's got big numbers. That's the number written on the back." He showed the number to the American who punched it in to his own, a state of the art, miniature mobile videophone.

"And what's your number, Sgian?"

"I don't carry a phone," Sgian replied. The American was taken aback.

"And there's another first. A boy without a cellphone. Tell me about your name."

MacKenzie replied. "It's Gaelic for 'knife'. It suits him; he's sharp and swift."

"We have a name back home just like it. Blade," the American said.

The PA loudspeaker squawked, "The buffet will close in twenty minutes. Anyone wishing to purchase drinks, snacks or ice cream should proceed to the buffet car now."

The American's mobile rang. He listened, said nothing then pocketed it. He looked at his watch, took a banknote from his wallet and turned to Sgian, saying, "How d'ya fancy some ice cream, Sgian?"

"Great. Three of the best coming up," the boy replied, taking the money.

As he was walking down the passageway an elderly lady wearing a brown coat with a fur collar, sitting in a seat with her back towards him, stood up. She started to make her way down the corridor. The train tilted as it went round a corner and the lady almost fell. Sgian steadied her. Without turning round she simply said, "Thank you, young man," then scurried towards the loo. Sgian was amused yet slightly puzzled.

'How did she know I was a young man? She never even looked at me?' he thought to himself.

Sgian made his way to the buffet car. Rain lashed the carriage windows in waves as the train struggled up a high glen before its descent to Inverness. He was the only customer.

"Well, young man, better in here than out in that," said the attendant, pointing out of the window. "Did wonders for sales of hot snacks. None left. But there's plenty ice cream."

"Three large ice cream cones, please," replied the boy.

"You want the Alpine specials?" asked the attendant.

"Yes, please."

He paid and took the three cones with massive peaks of ice cream and chocolate.

"Hang on to them, but keep your tongue at the ready in case the train stops suddenly," said the man with a big grin.

Sgian turned to leave the buffet with the ice cream Alps. The attendant pulled down the shutters. The train was slowing down. The boy heard fluttering behind him. He turned and saw a large streaked-brown bird with ears like horns, a bald patch on top of its head, a beak like an ice pick and vicious talons. Then he noticed the strangest thing. It had a tiny mobile camera phone against one ear.

"Ooo-hu. Chuckle, chuckle." It jumped towards him.

The lights went out.

5

reen crusts on city trees. Grey, woolly carpets on heathland.
Scarlet cups on peat bogs. Time stains and scribblings on stone
walls. Chewing gum spots on pavements. Black and orange patches on
seashore rocks. These are the lichens. A 'two in one' creature. Algae or
extremophile bacteria living between protective layers of flesh-eating
fungus. They thrive in extreme conditions: in freezing polar regions or
mountain tops, soggy tundra or submerged on seashore rocks. Some even
thrive in polluted areas. They can withstand temperatures from −196 to
+100 degrees C. They are unaffected by radioactivity. Lichens reproduce
by airborne spores or grow into new colonies if a part of the structure is
broken off and carried elsewhere. They can live for millennia, often in
suspended animation, an adaptation known as 'cryptobiosis'.

In a distant solar system, the planet Ianuarius has a dark side. Heavy
clouds of steam, carbon dioxide and methane cover a barren, black
lichen-covered rocky landscape. On the light side of the planet a runaway
greenhouse effect is progressing. Lichen invade and consume vegetation.
Air-breathing creatures are dying off. Attempts to regenerate the
atmosphere by harvesting phytoplankton from other planets have failed.
The last few survivors were attempting to create an energy source to
renew the atmosphere. The experiment ended when a volcanic eruption
occurred. It launched a meteor into space. It reached Earth in AD 140.

In 2005 the European Space Agency sent a rocket into space. The
Foton M2 satellite carried a sample of green lichen. It passed through a
cloud of particles that had been released from a massive volcanic eruption
on Ianuarius two millennia earlier. On its return from orbit the satellite's

18

titanium shell had been damaged. Of all the experiments on board, only the lichen survived, although its colour and bulk had changed. Biological and chemical studies suggested a metamorphosis had taken place. This was observed by one scientist, but not reported.

6

"Don't like the look of this," said Sgian. He ran in the dark. Fluttering getting nearer. He collided with a bony body and was enveloped in musty, smoky-smelling sleeves. The breath was squeezed from his lungs. A bony hand with sharp nails gripped one of his shoulders. He was pushed towards the carriage door, still clutching the ice creams, now coalesced into a sort of massive mountain on stilts. His captor inserted a key into the carriage door. Several things happened in quick succession. The train entered a tunnel. The communication cord was pulled. The train screeched and shuddered as it decelerated. The eagle owl behind squawked.

"Fancy an avalanche?" the boy shouted as he thrust the ice creams up into the darkness of his captor's hood.

The door was being opened. There was spluttering and sneezing. The restraining grip loosened. Sgian ducked and threw himself away from the door, his damaged knees taking another beating. The boy felt a blast of cold, moist air from behind, followed by distant rumbling and bubbling sounds. More spluttering from the assailant.

The boy scrambled on all fours into the darkened coach. He heard murmurs of discontent from passengers jolted out of their seats, dreams or holiday reading. He rummaged in his sporran for the penknife torch. The red light guided him to his seat. The carriage lights went on. The train started to move. A guard rushed down the passage.

MacKenzie looked across at the boy, saying, "Well, that was all a bit sudden. What happened?"

"A narrow escape, thanks to ice cream," said the boy with a smile.

The gardener looked puzzled. The American, sitting further forward and concentrating on the guard's activity in the corridor at the end of the coach, heard Sgian's voice, turned to look back and did a double take.

"What…! How…? You're here!" He regained his cool. "Well, blow me. How d'you get back here in the dark? You've got cat's eyes."

Further down the carriage the elderly lady in the brown coat was talking to a youth wearing a baseball cap. He turned and looked straight at Sgian.

The guard came back up the passageway, explaining what had happened.

"Sorry for that delay, folks. A most unusual occurrence. The torrential rain must have led to flooding and a mudslide through a hole in the tunnel. A door blew open and triggered the emergency stop. The passageway filled with mud. Fortunately, nobody was in the passage at the time. We'll still arrive in Inverness on time."

The guard continued on along the carriage and Sgian closed his eyes. He was knackered.

7

"**W**e are now approaching Inverness where the train terminates. Please ensure you take all your belongings when you leave." The announcement awoke Sgian.

At Inverness station MacKenzie and Sgian left the American, wishing him the best of luck in his 'Nessie' hunt. Sgian delayed MacKenzie in the station to see if the 'hoodie' had survived. There was no sign of him.

A stooped elderly lady, using a stick, hobbled towards them. He recognised the brown coat with its fur collar, but not the bespectacled face, partly hidden under a wide-brimmed hat. Handing a bag of chocolates to Sgian she said, "Thank you for helping me." She walked off.

"Been doing good deeds while I slept, Sgian?"

"Strange how she recognised me. She never saw my face on the train."

He put the chocolates into his bag and watched the lady walk to the station entrance. As she climbed into a waiting taxi, Sgian had a fleeting glimpse of a subtle change. She was almost like a cat pouncing on its prey.

The taxi door closed. A dramatic transformation took place. Hat, wig, spectacles and nose were removed. A tall, red-haired woman emerged. Half of her face was scarred and one side of her mouth twisted downwards. She spoke with a young, authoritative voice. "Airport. Fast." She sent a text message: 'Brother D. failed to deliver. Alternative steps taken. Subject of Internet search located. Dr Omar Aboud. Egyptian astrochemist. Owns chocolate factory in Switzerland. Consultant for the European Space agency. Links with Egyptian cult. Seeks religious relics. Believes located north-west Scotland.'

A reply was received almost immediately: 'Tell him to call me. Shall arrange meeting on *Highland Warrior*.'

8

After a night in a bed and breakfast MacKenzie and Sgian joined a bus queue. The baseball-capped man, carrying a stained holdall, approached MacKenzie.

"Is this for Poolewe?"

"Aye. Would you be going to work in the hotel?" MacKenzie asked.

"No. I'm joining a fishing boat as cook," said the youth, lighting a thin, half-smoked cigarette.

MacKenzie and Sgian boarded the Westerbus bound for Poolewe. They travelled through spectacular countryside. Deep, dark glens, high rugged mountains and countless lochans reminded the boy of his favourite adventure story. The bus descended a steep, single track road, stopping occasionally in passing places for on-coming vehicles and frequently anywhere to let sheep and wild goats cross.

As they drove by a huge loch dotted with small wooded islands, Sgian thought the landscape looked strangely familiar.

"What's that loch?" he asked.

"That's Loch Maree. It's very deep. They say it used to be a sea loch," MacKenzie replied.

Suddenly, the bus swerved and shuddered to a halt, its horn bellowing. Sgian banged his head against the seat in front. MacKenzie was thrown out of his seat, as were other passengers. The driver roared.

"What the…? Where do you think you're… going!!!!!?"

Up ahead, Sgian saw the reason for his sore head sitting with its bonnet in the loch. A small car had tried to overtake the bus on the single track road. Two men, getting out, stepped straight into waist-deep muddy water. Each man had his own personal cloud of midgies. The bus driver jumped from his seat and ran down to the lochside.

"Let's see if we can help," said MacKenzie. They followed the driver. Sgian recognised the men in the water.

"They're the men I heard talking about the Stone of Destiny in the station," said the boy.

"They'll no find it in the loch," MacKenzie replied, chuckling.

The other passengers watched from the bus. Except 'baseball cap'. He quickly moved to the seats vacated by Sgian and MacKenzie. He opened both of their bags, spotted the chocolates in the boy's bag and helped himself. He pulled a small cloth sack from his holdall, untied a string and emptied its contents into MacKenzie's bag. He returned to his seat, made a call on his mobile and sat back to enjoy the chocolates.

At the water's edge the two men were being attacked from above and sinking below. They looked distinctly uncomfortable and embarrassed.

"So sorry. We will make right any injury or damage. We are from Norway. We misunderstood the proper use of the passing place. It is our first visit to Scotland and we are driving a vehicle unfamiliar to us."

"Well, sir," began the bus driver, having vented his wrath. He pointed at two fishing rods. They had been ejected from the car's rear window and were embedded like spears in the loch's muddy bottom. "You've chosen the right loch to start fishing in. But we do things in a more leisurely fashion in the Highlands. And, if I were you, I'd get out of that mire before the midgies eat you alive or the kelpie drags you under. I'll get in touch with Colin's breakdown service in Gairloch. He'll sort you out."

They left the wet, mud-stained, itching tourists and headed for the bus. Sgian was last in line and caught sight of something moving in the clear water close to the shore. A striped green, yellow and brown creature. It seemed to smile then disappeared.

"Must have been a water kelpie," he thought.

"Sgian! Come on before we leave without you," shouted MacKenzie.

"Coming," the boy replied as he ran up the bank.

"What is a kelpie?" asked Sgian as he took his seat.

"A long-necked water dragon. They say it appears once every seven years and drags people and boats to the bottom of the loch. Nobody swims in Loch Maree. My father thought he saw one during a storm," MacKenzie replied.

The bus journey continued.

"Tring-tring! Tring-tring!"

It sounded like a fire engine. MacKenzie awoke from his snooze. Sgian shook his head and turned to look at him. MacKenzie took out his massive phone.

"Hello. Who is that?" he said slowly.

Sgian could hear the caller clearly. It was the American. MacKenzie turned the volume up. Everyone in the bus could hear it.

"Hi! It's Ollie. How are you doing? Just called to see how your trip was going."

He told the American they were on the bus bound for Poolewe.

The American continued, "I've just reached Loch Ness. Like I always imagined. Dark hills, dark woods, dark stony beach, dark brown water, deadly quiet. Not a soul apart from a million midgies." Everyone on the bus laughed. "Looking forward to exploring your mystery island. I'll give you a call..." The phone cut off.

"Must be out of range," said MacKenzie. He put his phone away, saying, "A considerate man, don't you think, Sgian?"

The boy nodded, but he wasn't so sure.

MacKenzie reached for his bag. "All this excitement's given me a thirst. Fancy a drink?"

Green, yellow and brown stripes came to Sgian's mind. He shouted. "Don't touch it!"

MacKenzie's hand was already inside.

"Owwwch!" he yelled. There were two bleeding pinpricks on his wrist. "I've been bitten. I feel dizzy..." His words became slurred and he slumped forward.

Sgian opened a window and threw the bag out. A green, yellow and brown striped snake wriggled in the air as it fell towards the loch. A dark shadow moved rapidly along the shoreline. A golden eagle grasped the serpent's head and flew off. MacKenzie was gasping for breath, his face red and swollen.

"Stop the bus! MacKenzie's choking. He's been bitten by a snake!"

The bus screeched to a halt. Passengers were jolted out of their seats. The sudden stop helped the boy pull MacKenzie to the floor. He was now unconscious. Sgian started mouth-to-mouth resuscitation. The driver came back to help.

"Keep going, lad. I'll call for an ambulance." After a few moments he said, "He's out for the count, but still has a pulse. I'll take over with the breathing now."

A screaming siren announced the arrival of the ambulance.

"That was quick," shouted the driver between breaths.

Sgian took over. The ambulance driver stepped onto the bus. He looked surprised at seeing the boy.

The bus driver said, "Where's Rory? I've no seen you before. How did you get here so quickly?"

"Oh, I'm new. He took ill. I was on my way to Inverness when I heard your call."

"This is a desperate emergency. If ye don't know the roads you'll never get to the hospital in time. I'll drive. You keep the CPR going." He turned and shouted to a man at the back of the bus, "Jimmy. Can ye take the bus on to Poolewe?"

"Surely, Alfred," he replied.

"I need someone else to help wi' the CPR," said Alfred.

A mountain of a man came forward.

"I've done the first aid course, Alfie."

"Good on ye, Jock. Could ye bring the stretcher out?"

Jock returned carrying the stretcher as if it were a newspaper.

"It smells a bit like a fish market in the ambulance. Did Rory say who the salmon were for?" he said to the ambulance driver.

The replacement ambulance driver hesitated. "Eh? Oh yes. He told me to take them to the Station Hotel."

Sgian noticed the sceptical look on Jock's face.

They lifted MacKenzie onto the stretcher and took him to the ambulance. The ambulance, siren blaring, raced off. Jimmy sat in the driving seat and turned to the boy, saying, "You did well. MacKenzie's a great friend of mine. I hope he'll be alright." He spotted the chocolates in the boy's bag and added, "Mind if I have one of these? I'm a bit peckish."

"Help yourself," the boy replied and sat down beside the driver.

The bus set off. It crawled up a long, steep hill, leaving Loch Maree behind. Ahead, in the late afternoon sun, the Atlantic Ocean glistened. Gentle waves lapped a pebble and seaweed-strewn shore. Poolewe sat peacefully in the distance.

"That's the finest view in all the world, Sgian," said the driver as the bus reached the summit and started to descend a long, steep hill lined with tall bushes down to a narrow bridge at the entrance to the village.

"That bridge crosses a tiny part of the Atlantic Ocean at high tide," said Jimmy, smiling.

The bus swerved. The driver's speech was slurred.

"I feel dizzy. I think I'm gonna pass out."

He slumped forwards. The bus was hurtling towards a deep ditch on one side of the road. Sgian pushed the unconscious man back against the seat and grabbed the large steering wheel. He pulled the wheel down with all his might. The bus slewed across to the other side of the road. Jimmy's foot was jammed on the accelerator. The boy pushed and pulled on the wheel. The bus zigzagged with increasing speed down the steep hill. He couldn't reach the brake. Screaming passengers were thrown about. The bus was out of control, hurtling towards a tight bend leading to the narrow bridge.

9

The ambulance slewed round hairpin bends, bounced over potholes, siren blaring and blue lights flashing. The two men in the back trying to keep MacKenzie alive were being thrown about, but managed to keep some sort of CPR going. But one of them had another idea.

"We'll soon be off the single track road. How is he?" shouted Alfred.

The ambulance driver turned and shouted, "His heart's going. Breathing's the problem. I'm about to relieve Jock." At that moment he was kneeling behind Jock with a hammer in his hand. Jock was squeezing a ventilator bag.

"Hold on!" shouted Alfred. A lorry thundered round a corner towards the ambulance. Alfred pulled the steering wheel over. The ambulance mounted the roadside verge on one side, tilting to an extreme angle. The lorry plunged into a deep ditch on the other side. The man with the hammer was thrown violently across the ambulance and the large wooden box, packed with frozen salmon, conveniently finished the job by crashing with great force onto his head. Eighteen stone of muscle, fat and bone kept Jock rock-steady throughout the near collision. He didn't let up for one moment in his efforts to keep MacKenzie alive. He was totally oblivious to what might have been.

Alfred didn't even look back. He floored the accelerator and the vehicle took off again. Jock looked up and saw the unconscious man, his head beneath the fish box and still clutching the hammer. He murmured, "Now there's a thing. I thought there was something fishy about you."

10

The bus approached the corner at high speed. Sgian pulled on the steering wheel with all his remaining strength, but knew it was impossible.

"Brace yourselves!" he shouted.

Suddenly, a girl on horseback emerged from behind some bushes just before the corner. Rider and horse heard the bus and turned to look. The girl was thrown as the horse reared and galloped off. She lay, with a look of terror, directly in the path of the oncoming bus. Sgian wrenched the wheel in the opposite direction. The bus slewed round and tilted onto two wheels. The girl, only a few yards ahead, screamed as it rushed past her and crashed through a gate into a field. Deep, thick mud brought it to a halt. He switched the engine off.

"Phewwwww…!" Sgian blew out a long breath, which he'd been holding for the last minute. Cheers broke out from the other passengers who rushed forwards.

"Well done, lad. You're a star. Schumacher has nothing on you!" someone shouted.

The girl, obviously in pain but managing a faint smile, appeared at the door of the bus. She was holding one arm against her chest. With a look of amazement on seeing the boy driver standing beside the slumped body behind the wheel, she said, "Wow, that was close. What can I say? A big thank you. I'm Fiona Bellamy."

Sgian stepped down from the bus. She gave him a one-arm hug. He was shaking inside.

"I'm Sgian. Luck was good for all of us," he replied, unable to stop himself gazing into her hazel eyes. "That looks painful," he added, pointing to her arm.

"Oh, it's not broken. Just taken a jolt. I'm used to falling off Duke. He's jumpy. I'll see the doc in his surgery. It's just down the road. See you later perhaps?" she said, turning to go.

"Yeah. Great," he replied.

She smiled and walked away.

A very large policeman with a ruddy complexion, a black moustache and spectacles approached, leading the horse.

"Well, that was a near thing. I saw it as I was coming out of the post office. I'm glad you're still in one piece, Miss Bellamy. I caught Duke down by the river. Now, can anyone tell me what's been going on?" he asked.

"Let's go, Duke," said Fiona, rubbing his nose. "Thanks again, Sgian," she added before leading her pony away.

Sgian introduced himself to the policeman and described events from when MacKenzie was bitten by the snake.

The policeman shook the boy's hand. "Well done, lad. The folks round here won't forget this. I'm Ian Cross, by the way. I got word from Alfred that he was taking MacKenzie to hospital and I've told his mother. It sounds serious," he said.

Jimmy was coming round as two passengers carried him from the bus. He looked perplexed.

"I feel like I've got a hangover. It must have been these chocolates. Better give them to the police, Sgian. I think they've been drugged."

"A woman gave them to me at the station," said Sgian, realising he'd been the intended victim.

The policeman's mobile rang. He listened for a moment then said, "I'll be over shortly." He turned to Sgian and Jimmy. "I've just heard that Rory, the ambulance driver, has just broken out of a shed where he'd been gagged and tied up by someone. Whoever drove the ambulance to the bus had some other agenda. Just as well Alfred took it to Inverness. I'll get in touch with the hospital to make sure they arrived, and find out about that character."

One passenger remained on the bus. The baseball-hatted individual was just stirring from a deep sleep. He stood up, shook his head and pulled his cap down over his eyes. He stepped down from the bus.

"End of the line, sir. Looks like you slept through all the excitement. Where are you off to?" asked the policeman.

"Oh, yes. I'm meeting someone who'll take me out to a fishing boat.

I'm the cook," he said. He picked up his holdall and walked off.

"Have the Doc check you over, Jimmy. We'll go along to the MacKenzie croft now, Sgian."

The sea loch was calm. A pale blue sky had high mackerel clouds.

"Croo-ee," a curlew called.

"Kleep, kleep." A black, white and orange flash of oystercatchers swooped over the rocky beach.

"Stormy weather ahead," said the policeman.

Sgian was lost in thought.

"You've earned your supper tonight, Sgian. Jessie MacKenzie makes the finest scones in the village. She'll be glad of your company, what with the worry about her son. There's another lodger staying at the croft. A Professor Anna Sterne from Norway. She's some sort of geologist doing research. Here we are," said the policeman as they approached a white cottage. A plume of blue peat smoke drifted up from the chimney. Two hens scurried clucking round to the back of the house.

"That smell tells you you're in the Highlands. It gives a special taste to the tea – and the whisky," he added with a smile.

The door was opened by a worried-looking white-haired lady. She had brown eyes, a weather-beaten face and wore a yellow and black MacKenzie tartan pinny over a green jumper and dress. Sasha, the Border collie, stood by her side. A sharp bark. Hairs bristled on her back. She moved closer to Mrs MacKenzie.

"Come on, Sasha. What's got into you? This is Sgian, MacKenzie's young friend."

The boy was used to dogs being a little wary of him. He never understood why. Cats took to him right away.

"Hello, Sasha," he said, putting his hand forward. Sasha sniffed then wagged her tail.

"How are you, Jessie?" said the policeman. "This lad has quite a tale to tell."

Sgian smiled, shook Jessie's hand and patted Sasha.

"I'll organise your transport to the hospital tomorrow. MacKenzie's getting the best of care. I'm sure he'll be alright. I'll have to be going now. I've a report to make out," said the policeman.

"Many thanks, Ian. I'll be ready first thing," said Mrs MacKenzie.

As the policeman walked out of the gate he was thinking that MacKenzie's life may be in the balance. He'd break it to her gently on the journey in the morning.

Sgian, Sasha and Mrs MacKenzie went inside.

11

A fishing boat ploughs through white-topped waves. Clouds are gathering. A sou'westerly wind is picking up. In the skipper's cabin a bald, ruddy-faced man with grey-green eyes, bulbous nose and black moustache examines a surgical instrument. An identical device lies in an open red suitcase. The man's name is Nochd Maree.

"The Pathfinder will revolutionize neurosurgery. Oliver Jeffrey would have achieved world fame if he'd lived to use it," he says with a smile.

Standing in the doorway is another man of identical stature, the same grey-green, lifeless-looking eyes, but with long black hair. A jagged scar runs across his neck. He wears fisherman's gear. His voice is like a painful whisper.

"Why must you pursue this boy? Your obsession will lead to disaster. And why didn't you leave the skipper with the rest of the crew on Gruinard Island, brother?"

"You will never understand. My brain is built for the second sight. And I know how it should be used. I brought the skipper along because he may be related to the boy. His name's Roderick Dubh. That could be useful," said Nochd.

His mobile rang. He recognised the call sign.

"Yes, Gail?"

"Dr Aboud wishes to discuss trading his lichen for information about Egyptian relics."

"Good work. We've prepared a site for planting on Nan Ron Slapach. That lichen is the perfect transplant drug. It will provide a new horizon for your special skills and a cure for our personal afflictions." He touched

32

his lips. "But tell me more about the relics he's interested in."

"I think it's a cover story. He's into cosmic energy research. The latest space mission returned with some highly reactive unknown substance. These so-called relics could be connected."

"Interesting. Perhaps there's another prize within our grasp. We play him along like the skilled fishermen we are. How are your plans for the boy and MacKenzie proceeding?"

"I met your new cook on the train. He's been paid to plant the viper and ensure the boy is drugged. MacKenzie should be breathing his last as we speak. But the boy... he's still wide awake." There was fear in the woman's voice.

Silence followed by heavy breathing as Nochd sought to contain his anger.

"Is it incompetence? Or does this boy really have such a powerful second sight that he leads a charmed existence?" he said.

The woman did not answer.

"A certain piece of his brain will be mine. One final trial, then the stage is set for our pioneering step. Return with all speed when you have our latest donor's brain cells. A new dawn in medicine is on the horizon. Curing dementia with animal brain transplants will bring us fame." He laughed. "It will give new meaning to the sayings 'wise as an owl' and 'an elephant never forgets'."

She gave a nervous laugh then said, "The helo leaves within the hour," and closed the call.

Another call came through immediately.

"Nochd here," he said.

"My name is Aboud. I am a chemist. Your colleague said you may have information about certain Egyptian relics," was the reply.

"And why might you be seeking Egyptian relics in Scotland?" asked Nochd.

"They were stolen from the temple of our Sky Goddess by some Christian monks. A stone you call the Stone of Destiny and a golden horn," said Aboud.

"Do you realise how much the Scots value the Stone of Destiny and the risk involved in taking it from this land?" said Nochd.

"I do. I also know that the Stone which was returned to Scotland is not the original. It lies hidden somewhere. The lichen I offer in exchange is unique. It may be an alien species. I run a great risk in taking it, my friend. What do you intend to do with it?" continued the Egyptian.

"I'm engaged in medical research in transplant and plastic surgery. Perhaps you've heard of Gruinard Island?"

"Yes," said the Egyptian.

"I acquired the island after its decontamination. A lichen had been used in experiments on seals. My ancestors have known that the lichen affected the behaviour of seals. The Ministry of Defence thought they might use it to train seals to be submarine spotters. But disastrous genetic and immune side effects occurred. Some seals gave birth to monsters. Irradiation enhances the anti immune effect of the lichen. It will permit transplantation of brain tissue between species."

"And you have been successful?" asked Aboud.

"Results are unpredictable. I'm convinced that cosmic radiation will create the perfect immunosuppressant."

"Very interesting indeed, Mr Nochd. This lichen thrives on methane. If I'm not mistaken, there is an island not far from you which has been volcanic. There will be high concentrations of methane at depth. An ideal place for propagation."

"As you suggest, we might usefully collaborate. My colleague, Dr Gail Kirk, is a plastic surgeon. She will give you a tour of our establishment. I have already identified the seeding ground for your lichen. I shall arrange a meeting shortly," Nochd replied and closed the call.

Nochd turned to the other man and said, "Ronachan, we are to be blest by good fortune. It has come to my notice that a certain Norwegian professor is looking for the Stone. And a Viking artefact has been taken from the Oslo museum. Perhaps that's the gold horn our Egyptian friend seeks. There's more to these relics than meets the eye."

"We know who can help us find the real Stone," said Ronachan.

Nochd nodded, saying, "I think your special skills are required, brother. You might even get the chance to avenge our stepbrother's death and your terrible injury."

The other man fingered his scar.

12

"**C**ome away in, Sgian. Sit yourself down and have some tea and scones. As Ian said, MacKenzie's in good hands so we'll just wait and see what tomorrow brings."

Footsteps came down the stairs and a tall young woman walked into the sitting room.

"Ah, here's the Professor. She's our other lodger who's come from Norway."

Sgian looked into the palest blue eyes he had ever seen.

"Hi," said the boy.

"I'm Anna Sterne. Very happy to meet you. I heard about the terrible journey and how you worked a bit of a miracle," she said, giving him a hug. He was taken aback, but it made him feel really good. "It's a bit like coming home here. I'm from a place by the sea and not far from mountains," she went on.

Mrs MacKenzie looked more closely at Sgian, saying, "My, my, that's a terrible bump you have on your head. Is it that trolley thing you've been falling off?" She pointed to the skateboard.

"Och, it's nothing. I slipped off the seat in the bus. I never fall off my skateboard," he replied, smiling.

Sgian enjoyed a new experience for supper. Fresh herring, home-grown potatoes, parsley and carrots, which Mrs MacKenzie said would be good for seeing in the dark. This was followed by trifle made with fresh cream and raspberries. Everything came from the soil and sea near the cottage.

"The herring are just like my mother made for us at home. It's truly home from home here. Now I understand why the Vikings liked this place so much," said the Professor.

35

As they were enjoying pancakes and tea, the Professor examined the tea tray closely.

"That's an interesting piece of wood. It looks very old," she said.

"You've a good eye, Professor. My husband was working on the new road along Loch Ness and found it washed up on the shore after blasting rocks. He used to say it was old enough to have come from the drowned village under Loch Ness."

"It certainly is old, Mrs MacKenzie. It could be from the steering oar of a Viking ship. Over a thousand years old, I'd say," replied the Professor.

"Now there's a thing! How did a ship get in there before the canal was built?" said the old lady.

The Professor looked pleased, saying, "I think you've just given me a vital clue to a puzzle I'm trying to solve. Would you mind if I took a photo?"

"By all means. We've had it now for over thirty years and never known what it was," said Mrs MacKenzie.

In an instant the Professor produced a tiny digital camera and snapped it from every angle.

Their host smiled, saying, "Loch Ness is full of mystery."

The Professor's eyes brightened.

"I'd be very interested in any stories, Mrs MacKenzie," she said, taking out a notebook and pencil.

Mrs MacKenzie thought for a moment then began.

"Well, there's the story about how it got its name. Long ago in a glen near Inverness there was an ancient well. They'd been told that something terrible would happen if it was not covered over after use. One day a young woman drew water from it and heard her bairn crying. She rushed off without covering it up and the water flooded the glen. For a long time after that folks would look for the glen and village, saying in Gaelic, 'Tha loch ann a nis'. That means 'There is a loch in it now'. The Gaelic words merged into Loch Ness."

The Professor was smiling as she scribbled her notes.

"That's pure gold, Mrs MacKenzie. Thank you so much. In just a few minutes you've given me more clues to my puzzle than hours of research in the Oslo Viking Museum."

"What about the kelpie in Loch Maree? MacKenzie said his father had seen it," said the boy.

"That's another story, and it could well be true, Sgian. Folks around here talk about a long-necked beast that appears for a few moments every seven years somewhere in the loch," said Mrs MacKenzie. "My husband saw something like that happen when he was fishing on the loch. It was a fine, calm day and suddenly huge waves appeared in the middle of the loch. Then the long neck popped up for a few seconds and disappeared. The water calmed down almost immediately."

"When was that?" asked the Professor.

"That was in 1971, the year MacKenzie started work at the Botanic."

The Professor smiled, saying, "We'd better keep our eyes open, then."

After supper Sgian, Sasha and the Professor went out into the garden. The sun was setting on a calm, blue-green sea.

"This is a perfect place for a working holiday," said the Professor.

"What do you do?" asked the boy.

"I'm a geochemist, which means I study the chemistry of rocks."

"Is that to do with volcanos and things?"

"Yes. Volcanos, meteorites and even a bit of archaeology. I've come here to look at a fault in the earth's crust. Now, let me ask you something," she said, looking at his kilt. "That's the most unusual tartan I've ever seen, Sgian. What clan is it?"

"It's the Maree tartan. My mother's family. Nobody knows anything about the clan. My Head's asked me to find out," the boy replied.

"Maybe we're in the same boat, Sgian. I lost both parents when I was very little and there's no other family. So I've been trying to trace the family history. It goes back to Viking times. And one of my ancestors came here."

"When was that?" asked the boy.

"Over a thousand years ago. I'm going to explore a ruined chapel at Laide. In the Oslo museum there's a reference to some stone carving to be found there. There might be clues about the Viking activities in these parts. Fancy a trip, Sgian?"

"Great. Could Sasha come too?" he asked. Sasha's bark provided the answer.

Mrs MacKenzie came out of the house and the Professor told her of their plan.

"Sasha will love that. I'll phone Morag MacDonald, the retired Gaelic teacher in Mellon Udrigle. She'll be able to tell you something about your clan when she sees the tartan, Sgian. So you can drop in to her cottage. It's not far from your ruin," said the old lady. "You've a real treat in store. Morag's quite a character. When she was a student, she and some friends broke into Westminster Abbey and brought the Stone of Destiny back to Scotland. The police recovered it but I think there's still a secret that only Morag knows," she added.

13

"I'm back, Mum!" Fiona Bellamy called as she stepped through the front door of 'Londubh House', the 18th-century stone-built, ivy-covered laird's residence on the bank of the River Ewe.

"I thought you'd got lost, Fi! Where have you been?" said Mrs Harriet Bellamy from the landing at the head of a creaky wooden staircase.

"I told you I'd gone riding on Duke, Mum. Sorry I forgot to write it in your notebook. My memory's maybe going like yours," the girl replied.

"Goodness me, Fiona! What in heaven's name's happened?" She'd seen the arm in a sling.

"It's just Duke playing up again. Though this time with good reason. Nothing broken. The Doc's seen it." She told her mother about the near miss. "That boy's quite something. He was pretty shaken up himself. And MacKenzie, who'd been bringing him here, took seriously ill on the bus. Could we have him over for a meal, Mum?"

"Of course, dear, but we'll have to hear what Omar has planned for the next few days."

"I wish you wouldn't keep calling him that. He's Dr Aboud."

"Now, now, Fi. He's been so kind and helpful since the accident. And your father thought a lot of him."

"I'm not as keen on him as you are, Mum. I'd be careful. There's something wrong I can't put my finger on."

"Oh why can't you be kind to him like your brother?"

"He's never given me a satisfactory explanation as to how the accident happened. I think it had something to do with his notebook. Daddy discovered something about an asteroid and some energy source.

Whoever stole it will never crack the code. I helped him work it out," said Fiona.

"Hello, girls. We're back." Dr Omar Aboud walked through the front door carrying fishing rods and three trout. He was followed by Fiona's younger brother Mike.

"We had a great time. I'm starving," said the boy as he ran through the hall towards the kitchen.

"I'm sure you'd enjoy fishing, Fi," said the Doctor.

"My name's Fiona, and I prefer more energetic activities," said the girl.

"That's unkind, Fi," said her mother.

"I apologise," said the man, "but I thought I knew you well enough after these difficult few months. Perhaps we could do a Munro or two together."

Fiona's eyes widened. She said nothing, just stared at the man. Her father had died climbing in Switzerland with this man. She was convinced he was in some way responsible. She would never go near a mountain with him.

He continued. "People were talking in the village shop about the accident. I met the Doctor. He told me how lucky you'd been. You take too many risks, Fiona," he added.

"Dad always said, 'life's all about taking risks'." With these words she quickly ran upstairs to her room.

"I'm sorry, Omar. She's headstrong and needs more time to adjust. She's so like Frank in many ways and was determined to follow in his professional footsteps," said Mrs Bellamy.

"Yes, my dear Harriet, I understand. We must be patient. Now, I must prepare for my meetings and trip to Switzerland."

"What meetings? Switzerland?" asked Mrs Bellamy with a surprised look on her face.

The man frowned then reached into her apron pocket and pulled out a notebook. He read from it.

"Here it is. 'Omar leaves for Zurich Wed. 15th.' You're even forgetting to use your aide-memoire, my dear. I told you, Harriet, Montez runs the family business but he's only 19 and still needs his father's advice from time to time. And I did mention meetings with a scientist who has a laboratory nearby."

The Egyptian went to his room, opened his laptop and sent an email:

'To Montez Aboud, Director, Xocochoc, Zurich, Switzerland.
1. Close to locating energy source. Recovery team recruited.
2. F. holds key to notebook.
Omar.'

14

After helping with the washing up, Sgian asked if he might go for a run on his skateboard along by the shore.

"The sea air'll do you a lot of good, especially after such a day. Why don't you take Sasha? MacKenzie always took her out in the evening." Tears came into her eyes.

"Don't worry, Mrs MacKenzie. He'll pull through. We'll phone the hospital now," said the Professor.

The old lady wiped her eyes and gave a little smile.

"You're both a great comfort to me. Off you go now, Sgian. Take MacKenzie's whistle. Sasha's a right one for running away after the seals."

It was windy and the waves were white topped. The boy rolled along the deserted seaside road. Sasha was far ahead on the beach hunting for seals. He spotted a motorboat heading for the shore. The baseball-capped man who'd been on the bus was working the outboard. A small terrier was yapping in the bow and a big bird was keeping pace with the boat up above. Sgian ran on to the beach to hide among some bushes. Gorse prickles are not kilt friendly!

'Baseball Cap' jumped ashore. A car drew up directly opposite Sgian's hiding place. A pair of white trouser legs stepped out of the car. A foreign-sounding voice called out, "Are you from the one called Nochd?"

"He's waiting on the fishing boat out there," was the reply.

"Carry this bag," said 'White Suit'.

Sgian watched the two men walk down the beach and climb into the motorboat. He saw that the Jack Russell had a purple scar on his head.

The dog looked straight at Sgian's hiding place and yelped. The boy was certain he heard the dog shout, "Boy watching. Bow-wow."

"Go get him, Jack!" shouted 'Baseball Cap'.

The dog growled and jumped ashore. It ran to the gorse bush and barked, "Grr, gerrout. Grr, gerrout!"

'Baseball Cap' was right behind and pulled Sgian out by his jacket collar.

"Well, what have we here? This is indeed a stroke of luck. Nochd will be pleased!"

Sgian was roughly dragged down the beach and thrown into the boat. The eagle owl with its camera attached hovered above. Sgian fell face down and lay still. An idea came to mind. The engine revved and the boat lunged into the oncoming waves. He heard the barking of seals accompanying the boat.

"The whistle might get someone's attention," he thought. He pulled it from his pocket and blew. The high pitch was easily audible above the sounds of the outboard motor and the crashing waves. A few moments later there was great commotion among the seals. He heard squealing, barking, thrashing of flippers and great splashing all around the boat. Sasha's head appeared at the side of the boat. The Jack Russell jumped towards her and snapped at her ear. There was a gush of blood and Sasha howled then turned and swam back to the shore. But something else was causing commotion among the seals. The boat almost stood on end. 'Baseball Cap' lost control. 'White Suit' lost his balance. A leather-bound notebook fell from his hand. The boat rolled. All four occupants slid into the water.

Sgian started to swim. He felt something take hold of his jacket sleeve and pull him away from the boat. It was Sasha. Sgian caught a glimpse of 'White Suit' swimming back towards the boat. His jacket was streaked with red. A mauled dead seal floated by.

The boy and Sasha swam ashore. He looked at Sasha's ear. The terrier had torn a chunk out of it, but the bleeding had stopped. He found his wheels in the gorse bush and the pair sped back to the village. Running against the wind helped dry both boy and dog by the time they reached the MacKenzie house.

Sgian told Mrs MacKenzie that a terrier had snapped at Sasha but did not mention his near kidnap. The boy went upstairs to bed. Just as he was dropping off to sleep there was a thump and fluttering outside the bedroom window. Sgian opened heavy eyes but saw nothing.

15

On the fishing vessel *Highland Warrior*, Nochd and his brother followed events on the motorboat transmitted from the owl's head camera.

"That boy's escaped yet again! Eoin must follow him day and night. I will have him!" said Nochd, clenching his fists. "Fish our guest out of the water. But give greater priority to saving the lichen," he added.

"What happened?" said Dr Omar Aboud, having exchanged his wet, pink-streaked white suit for fisherman's gear. He was clutching a mug of steaming strong tea.

"Something attracted the beast to the boat," said Ronachan.

"What beast?" asked the Egyptian.

"A giant rogue seal from a family of mutants," said Nochd.

"That boy used a whistle just before the attack. And who was he anyway?" said Aboud.

"He's a boy with a very special talent whose ancestors wronged my family," Nochd replied.

Aboud was curious, but something in his host's tone forbade further questions.

"Now, if you care to look at the monitor. I have surveillance cameras installed on both islands. You can enjoy a guided tour of my surgical unit and lichen production plant while we proceed to more comfortable surroundings on Gruinard Island. We are heading for a monastery established by my ancestors who were made outcasts centuries ago. But science has replaced religion. Following your suggestion that we plant the lichen in a methane rich atmosphere, I have selected a rock formation high in the volcanic island," said Nochd.

The first image was of a helo landing pad within the rim of the extinct volcano. Banks of mist floated by, close to the summit. The camera was directed down a steep rocky slope inside the mountain and zoomed in on red and brown lichen-covered crags dotted with rowan bushes, clumps of heather and moss. A large rock face came into view. A thin film of water trickled over its surface. Grey-green mist hung in the air. There was a small ledge running across the face. Two figures, on tiptoes, were clearing moss from the rock. Wisps of smoke arose from the small containers each man carried around his neck. Smoke was inhaled with each breath. The camera panned down showing a sheer drop.

"These are two long-term patients, now employees. The smouldering lichen has narcotic properties. They're permanently spaced out, don't get vertigo and the midgies don't bother them. They'll plant the lichen today. Padraig and Tormod are brothers who volunteered for an experiment. The owl brain transplant wasn't my greatest success. They weren't the brightest before. Now they really are bird-brained but have a remarkable perching ability."

"Have you had any successes?" asked Aboud, raising an eyebrow.

Nochd was not troubled by this implied criticism. "The effect of a brain transplant is immediate. Even before leaving the theatre the client is aware of the result. I have many satisfied, intellectually enhanced clients."

"And how do you select your patients?" asked the Egyptian.

"I prefer to call them clients. Most of them are healthy, just vain or ambitious or paranoid or dim. But all of them have to be exceedingly wealthy. Can we talk about the lichen? I must have your assurance that no one else knows of its interesting properties and that I will own the entire specimen," said Nochd.

"No one else has been involved in its aftercare following its return to earth," said Aboud, nodding.

"And are you sure it will grow? And how quickly?" Nochd asked.

"It will require some time, perhaps a week, to settle in. It should double its mass within a month," replied Aboud.

"Excellent. Dr Kirk will take you to the island when she returns from Edinburgh. We are about to land on Gruinard Island where you will enjoy some real Highland hospitality," said Nochd.

"Just one question, Mr Nochd. You have the lichen; when shall I have the relics?"

"We are very close to acquiring them," was the reply.

Something in Nochd's manner raised questions in Aboud's mind. Would Nochd keep his word? He would require a Plan B.

Within twenty-four hours of being planted, the one-metre-square specimen of black lichen covered an area greater than ten square metres. The nearby rowan bushes had berries the size of apples. The trunks were no longer visible having been absorbed into the expanding alien.

16

The following morning Sgian and Sasha went to the front door after breakfast and found the Professor preparing her satchel for the day's work.

"Map, camera, paper and pencil for rubbings, a rope in case we need to do any climbing, sandwiches and juice for both of us from Mrs MacKenzie," she said.

Sasha barked.

"And, of course, Sasha's biscuits," she added, smiling.

Mrs MacKenzie waved them off at the front gate. The three set off in the Professor's hire car.

"First stop, Morag and your tartan mystery," said the Professor.

They stopped outside a small pink croft house. A rowan tree grew by the front gate. Rose bushes in flower and rhododendrons awaiting next spring lined the path up to the front door.

"Mmm... that's a wonderful scent, isn't it?" said the Professor.

Sgian nodded but he was more excited by the smell of the sea not more than a few hundred yards away. Sasha's nose was hunting under the bushes for more interesting aromas.

A small, white-haired, bespectacled woman opened the door.

"Come away in. I've been expecting you. It's Anna and Sgian, isn't it? I'm Morag. You're just in time for some of my oatcakes and honey," she said with a West Highland lilt.

When they were seated and enjoying the tea and oatcakes, Morag's eyes brightened.

"Now there's a sight for sore eyes. I haven't seen that tartan since I was a little girl, Sgian. Its colours are unique. The crottle that gives the green only grows on Gruinard."

Sgian and the Professor looked puzzled.

"What's the crottle?" asked the young woman.

"Oh, you call it lichen. It grows in peat bog," replied Morag. "I last saw this tartan over sixty years ago. A woman from Gruinard Island brought a tartan plaid to our house. She wanted to make kilts for her family and came to ask my mother how best to cut it. The Gruinard people kept very much to themselves. Could that have been your family, Sgian?"

At that moment he realised no one could help explain his mother's disappearance.

"I don't know," he spluttered, showering bits of oatmeal everywhere.

"No one knows what happened to that woman's family. They left the island in the 1930s. There's only a monastery there now. The plaid was woven by the womenfolk of the Maree Clan and was found at the foot of a steep gully on the mountain you can see from here." She took them to her kitchen window and pointed. "That's Bein Aridh Charr, Hill of the High Pasture. The story goes that a young Maree girl, helping Bonnie Prince Charlie in his flight from Culloden, slipped on the icy rocks and fell to her death. A shepherd found her bones about a hundred years ago under some rocks. There was a sgian dhu in the bones of one hand."

The Professor spoke, "What's a skeendoo?"

Sgian piped up, "The sgian dhu's a black knife."

Morag smiled, saying, "And I'm thinking you were given that name because you're so sharp, Sgian. They were wrapped in the plaid," she continued. "No one can explain how the cloth survived. I think your kilt's made out of that plaid, Sgian."

The boy now understood how his kilt seemed indestructible, despite the punishment he inflicted on it!

"The Maree Clan originally lived on Isle Maree and protected the monks who built a chapel there. The monks had brought the Stone of Destiny from Egypt. The Red Priest, Maelrubha, was head of the order."

"What's special about the Stone?" asked the Professor.

"Oh, it's said that the monks, who found it in an Egyptian tomb, believed it to have been used by Jacob as a pillow. Anyway, it has symbolic significance for us Scots. Our kings were crowned on it until it was stolen by the English."

"Then it was brought back to Scotland, wasn't it?" asked the Professor.

"It was that. After a struggle," replied the teacher with a smile.

"Mrs MacKenzie said you had a hand in that," said the Professor.

"Well, that's true. We took it from under their noses. The police caught up with us, but not before we'd substituted a lookalike for the real Stone."

"So the original is still in Scotland?" asked the Professor.

"Oh, it is that, and not very far away," she said, pouring out more tea. Turning to Sgian, and obviously wishing to change the subject, Morag said, "I'm sure you're from the Maree Clan, Sgian. You've the look of a Highland boy. You might be the last of your clan and have the only piece of Maree tartan in the world."

"What's second sight?" Sgian asked.

Morag smiled.

"The Maree Clan was blessed with a seer in every generation. It was someone who could see into the future. The Maree seers could also look back to the past. It was said that the gift was something to do with the colours of the tartan." She gave him a curious look and said, "Why do you ask, Sgian?"

"Oh, it's just something I read about Highlanders," he replied. But he could hear his father's words.

"And where are you off to now?" asked Morag.

"I've been told there's something interesting to see at the Laide Monastery ruins," the Professor replied.

"You'll know it has links with Loch Maree and Vikings, Professor. Followers of Maelrubha built that chapel with the help of some visiting Vikings," said the teacher.

She waved them off from her front door.

As they got into the car the Professor said, "You know, Sgian, it's a remarkable coincidence that both of our quests are linked. I think we're going to make a good team." She took a postcard from her pocket and showed it to the boy. "That's the village I live in. I'll write the address on the back. You'd enjoy a holiday there and I'd love to show you around."

"That would be brilliant," he said. For a second or two he saw what looked like a black cloud rolling down a mountainside. He blinked. The image was gone.

"And the Highland boy can show me some of Scotland now," was her reply.

They drove to a headland looking out to the Atlantic Ocean. White-topped waves rolled into a sandy beach below. Gruinard Island sat in the sea looking like a humpback whale.

"There's the ruin among these trees, Sgian," said the Professor.

They walked down a sandy path. The monastery was a pile of rubble. Sheep munched grass growing between stones. They paid little attention to the visitors. A remnant wall was still standing.

"The builders didn't do much of a job here," said Sgian.

"Well, it is over a thousand years old. Most of our houses won't last a fraction of that, Sgian. Carvings last longer than books. It's Torridonian sandstone. Very weather resistant, unlike the mortar they've used."

"What should I look for?" he asked.

"Carved drawings. They're like the fingerprints and thoughts of those who've been here. Why don't you give Sasha a little exercise first? That beach looks good for a game," suggested the Professor.

Sasha barked.

"I think she understood that. I'll be back in a few minutes," said the boy as Sasha ran ahead.

While the Professor searched about among the crumbling blocks of stone for signs of a carving, Sgian followed the dog towards a rise overlooking the beach. Sasha spotted some likely gulls to chase and bounded onto the beach barking. All her attempts to take off after them failed. When they returned to the ruin, Sasha buried a stick while the Professor showed Sgian a paper rubbing she'd made.

"I found two carvings. I think one shows a longboat carrying a rectangular shape with something like a handle on top. The other shows the handle flying above the rectangle. The boat is upending."

"And that zigzag. Is that lightning?" asked Sgian.

"Yes. And do you see that large cone beside the longboat?" asked the Professor. "Maps show that a volcanic island erupted out of the sea around the time the Vikings were here. Perhaps the lightning triggered an earthquake. I think the boat was sucked into the undersea quake. These events took place around AD 1200 when a series of earthquakes and volcanic eruptions rocked Europe. It was the beginning of the 'Little Ice Age' that lasted until the 1800s. We need a Little Ice Age now to reverse global warming. There's a fault in the earth's crust in this part of Scotland. It may involve Loch Ness, Loch Maree and run out to the sea." She took out a map of the area and drew a line through the two lochs. "Look, Sgian, it goes through a place marked as old mine workings and between Isle Maree and the shore of the loch. Let's explore along that line."

As they walked to the car Sgian saw a man looking towards them through a pair of binoculars.

17

A fine drizzle and breeze kept the midgies away. Mountain tops were shrouded in mist.

"We'll follow the track on the slopes above the loch first, Sgian. According to the map, it takes us through woodland to the old iron mine. We'll return by the shore and see Isle Maree."

The 'track' had been made by sheep and deer. The three explorers had much jumping, wading and scrambling to do over bogs, burns and big boulders. Sasha and the boy were thoroughly enjoying it. The Professor found it heavy going.

"Let's stop for a snack and some refreshment," she said. "I can see you love these hills. It's a bit like Norway, but I'm more at home on the sea, like my ancestors."

"D'you think they came here?" asked Sgian.

"I think they did. The Vikings wrote about sailing from the sea into Loch Maree and one account describes them helping Maree islanders to fight off raiders."

They descended towards the loch and, walking through woodland, reached a fork in the track. There was a sign pointing uphill: 'Danger. Concealed disused mineshaft. Entry forbidden'.

"There may be underground water in the mine. Let's go down to the loch and look for currents. That would suggest a deep channel."

At that moment Sasha picked up a stick and ran uphill.

"Not that way, Sasha!" the boy shouted. She turned back. The Professor set off down the path, Sgian ran after Sasha. He wrestled the stick from her, threw it and went to catch up with the Professor. She was some way

49

ahead and approaching a clearing among birch trees. Suddenly, he was aware of a musty, smoky smell.

"Stop! Stop! Professor…!"

He raced down the track shouting, then stopped. A few feet in front of him he saw a hole in the ground. Reeds and broken branches had been pushed aside where she had crashed through a concealed mineshaft. Her satchel was hanging on a branch. It had been wrenched from her shoulder. The warning sign had been turned, leading them into danger.

The boy lay down and looked into the hole. A steep, rocky slope disappeared into darkness.

"Prof! Can you hear me? Are you alright?"

No reply. Sasha joined him and barked.

"I'm going down. Don't worry, I'm coming to help," he shouted into the darkness. "Stay here, Sasha. Keep a lookout. Bark if anyone comes near."

He opened the Professor's bag and removed the torch and rope. He tied one end of the rope to a tree and threw the other end down the mineshaft, then sat on the edge of the hole.

"Well, at least it's dark down there. No problem. Here goes."

He climbed down a near vertical, rocky slope, stepping from one foothold to the next, torch in one hand, holding the rope with the other. He was aware of a familiar smoky, musty smell. Then he smelt rotting flesh.

The mineshaft opened out into a large cavern. Wisps of smoke drifted around the space as he reached the sloping floor. He saw the Professor's body. Large jagged rocks stood out like monstrous sharks' teeth. She lay on the only flat area amongst skins, entrails and bones.

"Wow! That was a lucky landing," he said, picking his way towards her. He switched on her torch. Her chest was moving.

"She's breathing," he said. "Prof! Anna!"

With these words her eyes opened. She was dazed but sat up and said, "It's good to see you, Sgian. Where am I?"

"You took the short cut."

She smiled, then sniffed, saying, "What's that appalling smell?"

"Dead meat and bones," he said.

She looked down at them.

"Seal skins. And the skulls have a hole in the top. Looks like a neurosurgeon's been busy or…" There was a sound.

They both looked round. Sgian shone the torch into the gloom. Black rocks formed the roof and walls of the chamber. Moulds and slime clung to the walls. Peaty water glistened as it dripped from cracks and crevices.

It was cold. The boulder-strewn floor sloped down into the gloom. He helped the Professor to her feet, gave her the torch then switched on his red light.

"How do you feel?"

"A bit stiff, thanks. But with your help I think I'll manage to get out of here. But let's have a quick look around first. This carnage is a bit frightening. I was about to say these holes in the skulls are just like those made by a walrus. It sucks out the brains of its victim." She paused for a moment and looked up. "Listen, Sgian! Do you hear it?"

"Running water," he replied.

She shone the torch in the direction of the sound.

"Yes. There's a stream. What's that?"

A white object was floating down.

"A hat. An American we met on the train had one like that. And he went to Loch Ness," said Sgian.

"Interesting," said the Professor, checking her compass. She looked at her watch as the hat drifted past. "If my theory's correct, that hat will go right out to sea. This smell's too much for me. Let's go," she added.

She shone her torch back towards the entrance. Something glistened.

"Look, Sgian!"

A silver chain lay on a bloodstained piece of dark grey cloth draped over a rock. The end of the chain was somewhere between the rocks. They picked their way towards it. The Professor put her hand to her mouth.

"Oh! A body. Or what's left of one."

Amongst the torn remnants of a hooded cloak they saw bones with some flesh still attached. The skull, like those of the seals, had a jagged hole in one side.

Sgian pulled on the chain. It was attached to a small, smoking metal cylinder.

"What is it?" he asked, handing it to her.

"It's an incense burner," she said, unscrewing the lid.

"I've smelt that stuff before," said the boy. He recognised the musty, singed hair aroma.

"It's lichen that's smouldering," she said, sniffing close to the fumes. "That's strange. I feel as if I'm floating. That smoke's intoxicating."

A shudder ran through the ground beneath their feet. There was a deep rumble then movement in the water nearby. The water bubbled and boiled as if an underwater explosion had taken place.

51

Whoosh!

A hideous-looking, slimy, dark grey-green creature erupted from the depths. A giant seal as big as a stretched limo. Large bloodshot eyes, huge snarling red lips drawn back over vicious white teeth. It surged towards them using two massive flippers. The boy knocked the burner out of the Professor's hand.

"Run! It's a giant walrus," he shouted, pulling her arm.

They scrambled over rocks in near darkness, apart from the tiny red torchlight. They reached the steep slope leading to the entrance. A greenish glow appeared. They both looked round. The beast was lumbering after them with its mouth wide open full of fish eyes. A luminescent glow shone from the teeth.

The boy was terrified but fascinated, shouting as he ran, "That thing's got headlights!"

He leapt from rock to rock behind the Professor. Despite her injury she was equally nimble. They spotted a glimmer of daylight from the mineshaft. The end of the rope was visible.

"There's the rope. Go up hand over hand; use rocks for your feet," he shouted.

A blast of foul-smelling wind hit him. The worst smell of vomit and rotten eggs he could imagine. A greenish-grey cloud seemed to envelope him. He felt dizzy. A hard, cold flipper smashed the side of his head and shoulder. A painful, slimy slap over one eye knocked him down. The giant beast's head filled the boy's vision. He looked straight into a staring eye and gaping jagged mouth.

A hissing sound followed by the outstretched claws of a wildcat hit the beast's head. A huge flap of bleeding skin was ripped open. A blood-curdling roar. The beast lurched back and rolled down towards the water's edge. The chunk of flesh hung from the side of its head. Blood poured from the wound. The beast was trying to grasp the loose flesh with its flippers.

"Well done, Tabby!" shouted the boy as he watched the cat bound up the steep incline and disappear out of the mineshaft.

Sgian picked himself up and scrambled over the rocks. He reached the foot of the mineshaft and looked up the near-vertical slope to the patch of daylight. The Professor was near the top. Sasha saw them and barked. Sgian grasped the rope and turned to make sure the beast had not pursued them. An astonishing sight met his gaze. In the ghastly, green glow from its mouth he could see the creature eating the large chunk of its own flesh still hanging from its neck.

The boy started his ascent. Halfway up the shaft a sound of movement came from behind. Before he could look round a sudden weight slammed him against the rocky side of the shaft. The appalling smell returned. An evil-looking open beak lunged at the rope above the boy's hands, its vicious teeth severing the line. Sgian let go and leapt to grip the rocks on the wall. He heard the heavy body behind him plunge and bounce its way down the shaft to the rocks below.

He scrambled up the rocky slope. The Professor pulled him out of the shaft.

"Globbed by a brain sucker. That's a first. But did you see that cat?" he said.

"You did well too, Sgian," said the Professor, shaking but still able to give him a hug. "Let's get out of here. There's no knowing what that thing's capable of."

They set off as fast as the Professor's limp would allow.

"Was that the kelpie?" the boy asked.

"It sure was. Like some sort of misshapen giant seal with a bad attitude. Remember what Mrs MacKenzie said about the long neck and giant waves? Maybe that was the baby and we've yet to meet the parents!"

Sgian cut a birch walking stick for the Professor.

Loch Maree was still and peaceful. A trout put her head above water to catch some supper. The mist had risen from the mountain tops and the sky had cleared of rain clouds.

"You're going to have a beautiful black eye tomorrow. Let's bathe it with some cold water from the loch," said the Professor.

He'd forgotten all about the 'flipper punch'.

"It goes well with the bump on my head," he said.

After a few cold compresses they set off.

"D'you think that thing's still alive?" Sgain asked.

"I don't know, but I'll tell you one thing, we're not going back to find out. I'll ask the policeman to organise a hunting party."

"I had a cat once," he said.

They walked on for some time, each lost in their own thoughts.

"I'll have to stop for a moment under these trees and rest this leg. Sasha looks like she wants to play," said the Professor.

Sunset. The western sky was ablaze with reds, pinks and gold. A V-formation of geese flew out to sea. A motor launch was moored some way off shore. The Professor pointed, saying, "I hired that motor boat to explore the shoreline. How about joining me tomorrow?"

"Great. Can Sasha come too?" he asked.

"Of course. She's part of the team."

He ran along the shore chased by Sasha. A flock of oystercatchers flew up, protesting. A heron left his rocky perch, flying lazily out over the smooth surface of the loch. A trout jumped to catch a fly. Sgian threw a stick into the water. Sasha ran to the water's edge, barking. She stopped, stood absolutely still, sniffed the air and the hair on her back bristled. The Professor walked over.

"What's she seen, Sgian?"

"I don't know. Have you noticed how quiet it is?" he whispered.

"You're right. And the birds have gone," said the Professor.

The dog turned and raced up the shore to the high bank. It hid in a clump of broom.

"Animals and birds can sense natural events before..." Her words were cut short by a terrifying shuddering of the ground under their feet.

"It's an earthquake, Sgian. Quick! Up onto the bank."

They had just reached the top when there was a deep roar behind them. A wall of water rushed from the middle of the loch. It surged up the shore and lapped at their feet, some two metres above the beach. They both stood staring at the receding wave and the ripples spreading out over the loch. After a few minutes the heron reappeared, a trout jumped and Sasha barked as she emerged from the bush.

"Wow!" shouted Sgian. "What happened?"

"That was a mini tsunami, Sgian. Let's get back to Poolewe. We've had enough excitement for one day."

"And I'm famished," said Sgian.

"Woof!"

"And so's Sasha," he added as the three set off.

18

Sgian was worn out. He went upstairs to the little bedroom. Pyjamas on, hot chocolate in hand, he sat on the bed and looked out of the window. There was a movement of bracken close to the house. A pair of almond-shaped eyes looked at him for a moment, then they were gone.

Loch Maree was so beautiful and peaceful. How could they have just been to hell and back? Must have been a dream. His eyes were getting heavy. He remembered Morag's story of the Maree Clan. Had they seen the creature he and the Professor encountered today? He looked at his kilt on the floor and the tartan seemed to dazzle his eyes. He fell back on the bed, sound asleep.

Then he was shivering in the dark. He stood ankle deep in snow looking out from a birch wood towards a long, dark loch. Clouds drifted past a full moon.

"Come and warm yourself, laddie!" someone shouted from behind.

He turned and saw a group of Highlanders in tartan plaids. They were huddled round a fire. He stumbled through the snow to join them.

"Have some hot broth, Maree boy!" A girl's voice. She crouched by the fire stirring a large pot. Her head was covered by a Maree tartan shawl. As she turned to give him a bowl of steaming soup her bright hazel eyes looked deeply into his. "How'd you like to keep me company on the walk over the hills to Loch Maree?" she said.

"You'll both be doing your Prince a great service if you get the message to the French ship at Poolewe," said a burly, bearded clansman.

Then a young blond-haired man, dressed in tartan trews and armour breastplate, spoke. Sgian thought he had a strange accent.

"The House of Stewart is indebted to the MacSorley and Maree families for their sacrifice at Culloden."

The Highlander and the young girl bowed their heads briefly in the Prince's direction. Sgian felt a warm glow flow through him as he finished the broth. The girl gave him a Maree tartan plaid.

"Wrap this round you. It'll keep the north wind out as we trek round Loch Ness. I'm Flora. What do I call you?"

"Sgian."

"Now there's a name with a story. You'll be the Seer's grandson?"

The boy looked puzzled.

"Och, you'll know soon enough," she added.

A full moonlight. Sgian had never seen so many stars. "What's that?" he said, pointing upwards. Bands of colour shimmered and danced in the sky.

"It's the Northern Lights," said the girl. "Mother Nature's lighting up our path."

Not a sound could be heard as they made their way over the snow-covered hills. Flora knew the way well even when the track was white. Sometime later an icy breeze made their faces tingle.

"A change on the way," said Flora.

The moon disappeared behind thick, dark clouds. It started to snow. They reached a promontory overlooking the loch.

"We'll shelter between these rocks," said the girl. They had to crouch to enter the space. "We've done well. You'll be seeing Isle Maree by sunrise."

She spread her plaid on the snow. They huddled together. It was snowing heavily.

A deep roar ripped through the still night. The boy jumped up.

"What's that?" he asked.

"A roaring stag. Unusual for this time of year. Something's disturbed him," the girl said.

Sgian caught a whiff of something musty. "Someone's coming!" he whispered.

"I can't hear…" She stopped speaking.

An approaching voice rasped, "Tracks in the snow, Captain!"

The boy and girl squeezed into a cleft under the rock. She dragged the plaid over the snow to smooth over their tracks. The squeak and crunch of feet marching seemed to be coming straight towards them.

"How can you can see through the smoke from that infernal thing you carry everywhere?" another voice called out.

"It concentrates the mind. They're not far ahead," was the reply.

"We'll catch up with them. Fleeing Jacobites are no match for the Dragoons. Lead on, monk!"

Sgian was frightened.

"Snow's covered the tracks. But I know where they're headed," was the rasping reply.

The two in hiding heard footsteps fade into the distance.

"You've the ways of the wild stag, boy. The wind's your friend," said Flora.

They stayed in hiding for a long time. Flora looked out from their shelter.

"The wind's died down and the clouds are clearing. I think it'll stop snowing soon. We'll make a start."

As she predicted, the moon lit their way through the thick snow. No sign of the soldiers' tracks. Dawn appeared behind them above the hills. Flora pointed to a dark shape in the loch some way ahead.

"We're almost there, Sgian. That's Isle Maree."

They walked along the snow-covered rocky shore of Loch Maree. The outline of croft houses and trees could be seen on the island.

Flora called out, "Mathair! Mathair, is Flora!" She waited, then called again. No reply. She pointed to a small jetty on the island, clearly visible now. There were two rowing boats on the shore.

"They've been taken from the island jetty," said Flora, looking at footprints in the snow. "Only Redcoats' prints heading away from the loch towards Poolewe." Tears ran down her cheeks as she looked toward Isle Maree. "If only we'd had the Seer..."

"What's that?" asked the boy.

"Someone who foretells. Our clan has been blessed with such a person each generation, but Culloden took your namesake from us, Sgian. We'll look in the Cave of Gold, the clan's secret hiding place. If anyone escaped from the Redcoats they would have hidden there."

She led the boy up a steep, icy, rocky slope. They walked along a narrow ledge. There was a sheer drop to the dark water below. When he looked back, she was gone. He took two steps and saw a narrow entrance to a cave. He went in. Flora was seated on a stone with sadness in her eyes.

"Come in, Sgian. There's no one here. The worst has happened."

Sgian knew what she meant. He remained silent but went to her and put his arms around her shoulders.

"What can we do? I want to help."

"Being here with me is a great help, Sgian."

The boy looked around the cavern. There was a small patch of daylight shining through a natural rock chimney. The walls were black and streaked with red-brown veins.

"Why is it called the Cave of Gold?" he asked.

"Long ago, monks of Maree brought a stone and a piece of gold from Egypt. They were kept in here. Vikings came up the loch with monks from Gruinard Island. After the visitors had been given a feast, the monks stole the stone, the gold and the Viking's longboat. The Viking chief gave chase and jumped onto the boat at a headland called Fox Point. A great lightning storm started an earthquake. The boat sank but the stone was thrown onto the shore and was saved. Sometime later it was given to the King of Scotland for safe keeping." She looked at her plaid and the boy's kilt then continued, "There may be no more of this enchanted cloth. We may be the last of the clan."

"You mean because it's hard-wearing?" the boy asked.

"There's more to it than that. It's said to give the second sight and a protection from bad spirits to a chosen few. Grandma told me the pattern and the green are special. The dye's from plants growing on rocks by Loch Maree and on Gruinard. There's a poem about it: 'Heather red, blaeberry blue, crottle green for the seer's een'. A legend says that the Maree plant stole the power from a water kelpie who came ashore and fell asleep among the rocks. The creature has been trying to reclaim it ever since. When the chosen one wears the Maree tartan, it brings out the gift."

She went to one corner of the cave and came back with a pot, some dry grass, birch twigs and flints. She started a fire for cooking.

"We'll have a little porridge then put right a wrong. The Jacobite cause has now become personal. We'll need help." Flora said this as she squeezed her hand between two rocks and pulled out a black knife.

"The womenfolk's sgian dhu. Its time has come."

Warmed through by the porridge, they set off following the soldiers' tracks in the snow. They approached a high mountain pass. Flora turned to Sgian, put her finger to her lips and whispered, "I hear voices. They've stopped. It's a tricky descent in the snow. We have work to do before then."

The 'work' took Sgian by surprise. They made the biggest snowball he'd ever seen and were just able to roll it close to the summit of the pass.

"You've got the shoulders and legs of a clansman," Flora commented. "Now we wait."

The sun shone. They heard movement on the other side of the pass.

"Let them get halfway down, then Mother Nature takes over," she whispered.

When the Redcoats were well down the steep gully, Flora and Sgian pushed the giant snowball to the summit.

"I can't see the monk. He must have gone on ahead. There are six soldiers. There were twenty-four women and children on Isle Maree. I'll be returning to the isle to bury them after my mission to Poolewe," said the girl wistfully.

At the summit they watched the straggling red line slither and stumble over the slippery surface. They could hear grumbling and shouting from time to time as feet unaccustomed to the Highland winter took punishment.

"The wind's in our favour again, Sgian. They won't hear it coming," she said. "Let it roll!"

The Redcoats didn't hear it coming until the last moment when a blast of cold air and a whoosh caused the last man to turn. His mouth opened, but no sound came as he was overwhelmed. They went over like dominoes but, unlike dominoes, they did not lie down but kept on tumbling after the snowball, which continued bounding down the gully getting larger and larger.

The two observers heard shouting and yelling as the Redcoats left shreds of red cloth and streaks of blood on the icy rocks and snow. Then all was silent.

"It is almost done, Sgian. The monk and the sgian dhu have to meet," said the girl. "Let's go!"

She took one step, then a giant bird flew down from a rock. But it wasn't a bird; it was the monk! He had a nasty-looking club in his raised hand and he brought it crashing down on the girl's head. Sgian watched helplessly as the two figures tumbled down the steep slope. He clearly saw the sgian dhu in Flora's hand bury itself in the monk's habit.

The boy shouted, "I'm coming to help!"

19

A masked figure silently opens a bedroom window, climbs in and tapes the sleeper's hands before she is fully awake.

"What do you want?" she asks in a quivering voice.

The intruder shows her a card with bold writing. Miss MacDonald reads the message and a look of terror crosses her face.

"Red Fox Point," she mumbles.

Her mouth is taped. She is taken out, bundled into a car and driven to Loch Maree. The intruder carries her to the water's edge. The Gaelic teacher mumbles some directions then something is forced into her mouth and the tape is reapplied. She is carried along the shore and up the bank. The two figures disappear behind bushes. The masked figure reappears and hurries off along the shore then dives beneath the smooth, dark surface of the water. A head appears close to a motor launch moored some way offshore. The figure hauls itself on board and moves towards the cabin. Shouts are heard from within. After a few minutes the boat's engine starts and it moves off.

20

Sgian awoke with a bump on the bedroom floor. As he clambered back into bed he looked around for Flora. Then he realised he'd been dreaming. Rain battered against the bedroom window.

There was a knock at the door. It opened and Mrs MacKenzie popped her head round.

"Are you alright, Sgian? I heard a bang on the floor. Breakfast's ready. After yesterday's escapade you'll be needing it."

"Mmm... smells great! Has the Professor had hers yet?" he asked.

"Oh yes. She's an early bird. Breakfast at six and off to Inverness. She said she had something to look up in the library."

The boy dressed quickly. He was tucking into bacon and eggs when there was a gentle knock at the kitchen door and Constable Ian Cross put his head round it.

"Sorry to interrupt you folks, but there's another problem. Something's happened to Miss MacDonald," he said.

"What's happened?" asked Mrs MacKenzie. "Sit yourself down, Ian. Have some tea while you tell us about it."

"Morag's neighbour took her milk in as usual this morning and found the house empty. No sign of her anywhere. We know she hasn't gone on the bus to Inverness. I know your visitor gets out early for a walk. Did she see anything suspicious?"

"It'll be evening before we'll know, Ian. The Professor went to the library in Inverness this morning," said Mrs MacKenzie.

"I'm organising a search party. Morag liked walking along the lochside," said the policeman. "There's something else I have to tell you, Jessie. MacKenzie's being moved to Edinburgh Royal Infirmary. He needs more specialised care than they can give him in Inverness. He's still unconscious."

Mrs MacKenzie was in tears and the boy's heart sank. He went and held her hands.

"He'll pull through, you'll see. We'll visit him together. And take Sasha, too!" he said.

"Thank you, Sgian. I think Ian would like you and Sasha to help find Morag. Is that not so?" she said, wiping her eyes with the corner of her pinnie.

"Indeed it is, Jessie. I'd be glad of a pair of sharp eyes," said the policeman, taking off his specs to clean them.

"You'll need this waterproof, Sgian. The sou'west wind's bound to bring heavy rain. I'll make sandwiches and a flask of tea for you both."

The sky was overcast. They felt a breeze as they climbed out of the Land Rover at the end of the track. Sasha was on her way. On the way down to the loch they both spotted the motorboat the Professor had hired. It bobbed about on the choppy water.

"That's the boat the Professor and I were going to explore the loch in," said Sgian.

"Well, today's not the day for small boats," said Ian.

A mist obscured the tops of all the surrounding mountains. It started to rain.

"Here it comes. Hoods up!" Ian shouted into the wind.

As they battled down to the water's edge through the downpour, Sgian looked towards the boat and saw someone in black straining on a rope running over the deck into the depths. The boat pitched and rolled in the waves.

"What's that person doing? Surely that can't be the Professor," shouted the boy, pointing to the struggling figure.

"Mrs MacKenzie said she's gone to Inverness. Who is it, then? And that looks like a fair old weight on the end of that line. See how the boat's keeling over?" said the policeman.

The rain was torrential. The wind whipped spray from the surface of the loch. Burns in full flood. Brown peaty water thundered down the hillside.

"I know where there's a cave," shouted Sgian, pointing towards the slope opposite an island.

"Then you know something nobody else knows, Sgian. I've been roaming these hills all my life and never seen or heard of one," said Ian.

The boy chose not to answer. He was thinking up an explanation.

The boy, followed by Sasha, found a narrow deer path winding up the steep, rocky slope. Water from an overflowing burn was tumbling over it.

"Mind how you go. It's slippy," the boy shouted over his shoulder. "This looks right," he said to himself. "I'm sure Flora went into an opening along this ridge."

"This looks very dodgy, Sgian. I think you're mistaken," Ian shouted.

The next moment, the boy recognised the large rock and stepped round it.

"Where have you gone, Sgian? Sgian?" shouted Ian. Then Sasha disappeared. "Sasha? Sasha? Come by, girl, come by!" he called out.

"In here!" shouted Sgian, putting his head round the rock. "It's well hidden," he added.

The cave was dark and damp. Peaty water ran down the walls. Sasha ventured into the gloom, carefully sniffing the air and the ground.

"Well, my lad, this is a revelation. You've really stumbled upon something. It's coming back to me now that there was a tale of a secret Jacobite hiding place somewhere along the shore. This must be it." He shook the water from his hat and glanced at his wrist compass. The needle was going crazy. "Look at that! Must be magnetic rock," he said.

Sgian looked around and found a small piece of red-brown rock. He put it in his pocket. Sasha growled from the depths of the cave.

"What have you found, Sasha?"

Sasha's growling echoed in the depths of the cave. The man shone his torch around the recesses ahead.

"There's a sack or something," said the boy.

"I can see... shoes. And I think I know who they belong to," the policeman shouted, moving forward quickly now.

They both reached the shape and joined Sasha who was sniffing all round it.

"I'm sure it's Morag," said the policeman.

He and the boy took out their knives and set about cutting ropes that bound the teacher. The sack was lifted off and a scarf removed from her mouth.

"Mercy me. That's a relief. Oh! Is that you, Ian? Wait till I get my specs on." She fumbled in a pocket and put on her thick glasses. "And Sgian, too! And here's Sasha! Well, that's a surprise. I was expecting the man in black again," exclaimed the elderly woman in a matter of fact way.

The two rescuers looked surprised. They helped her to her feet, then Sgian took the flask of tea from his sack, poured a cupful out and handed it to her. "That'll warm you through, Miss MacDonald. Then you can tell us your tale."

She started shivering. Sgian put the waterproof Mrs MacKenzie had given him around her shoulders.

"Thank you, Sgian. The shock's catching up with me. But this good strong tea'll put things right. Then I'll see if I can remember what happened," said Morag.

"Just take your time, Morag. We'll be here till it clears a bit," said Ian.

"That's better. Now, let me see. I was wakened by a sound. Someone wearing a hooded garment burst in. I couldn't see his face. I was pushed onto a chair and before I could ask anything he tied me up. Not a word when I asked what he wanted. Then the strangest thing. He took out a piece of paper with big writing on it. It said, 'Take me to the Stone of Destiny or you'll not see tomorrow. When I find it I shall release you'. Well, I thought, I'll tell him where it is. He may find it, but I'd a feeling he'd never be able to lift it. And anyway, he'll only have half of it. The Stone broke in two when we took it from Westminster Abbey. Only MacKenzie knows where the other half is."

The policeman smiled, saying, "So the stories are true. You've been keeping a secret for a long time, Morag! I never knew MacKenzie was involved."

"Well, it was for Scotland, Ian. MacKenzie was a great help to us. He was working at Inverewe Garden. Anyway, as I was saying, this character bundled me into a sack and brought me here. Wherever this is."

The policeman was shaking his head, saying, "You're a remarkable woman, Morag. Kidnapped, threatened with death and brought here. A cave nobody knew of. That is until Sgian found it. And you can stand here and say you were expecting that character to come back and release you?"

"You don't think he'd have left me here, do you?" she asked.

The policeman simply raised an eyebrow and said, "You're too trusting, Morag."

Sasha barked. Sgian heard something. "Sounds like a waterfall's just arrived."

Thundering, churning sounds of a great deluge echoed around the cavern. Following Sasha, they hurried to the entrance. It had stopped raining. They carefully made their way past the rock concealing the entrance. The roar of tumbling water grew louder. They saw white-topped waves and a boiling mass of water between Isle Maree and the shore.

"Looks like an underwater explosion. We'd better get up the hill," shouted Ian, his words barely audible above the water in turmoil.

Then Sgian shouted, "Look, the motorboat!"

The boat was pitching and rolling in the midst of the watery eruption. A black figure was just visible struggling at the helm.

Whoosh! A sudden upsurge of water under the motorboat. It rose twenty feet or more into the air. A sinister-looking shape appeared.

"The water kelpie!" shouted Sgian.

It was a huge dragon's head and long neck draped in slime and weeds. Water was gushing from its mouth. Within seconds the entire length of a Viking longboat surfaced. Through the spray the small motorboat could just be made out. It was being thrown about within the longboat like a toy in a bath.

"Now I've seen everything!" shouted the policeman above the roar of the water.

The longboat dived below the surface, taking the motorboat with it.

Silence. The loch became calm.

"There's someone in the water," shouted the boy, pointing to a head and flailing arms.

They rushed down to the beach. Ian reached into his sack, pulled out a rope, gave one end to Sasha and shouted, "Go fetch him, lass."

Sasha swam effortlessly to the head in the water. It kept disappearing below the surface then reappearing.

"He's near drowning. I hope she gets there in time," said Ian.

She did. The man grasped the rope and hung on. The Border collie's strength was unbelievable. She was actually pulling him! The moment she was near to the shore, Sgian rushed into the water, up to his waist, and took the rope. They pulled the man to safety. By this time he was barely conscious.

"Strange. This isn't the figure in black we saw on the boat just before it went down," said Ian.

"It looks like one of the Norwegians whose car ran into the water," said Sgian.

"The other one must have gone down with the boat," the policeman suggested.

"He's got hypothermia, whoever he is. Better wrap him up," said Morag.

"Are you alright there?" came a shout from behind.

It was Ian Cross mor, the even bigger brother of Ian. He was a deer stalker.

"Ian beag and Ian mor. The two of you are just what we need to get this poor soul to the doctor!" shouted Morag above the howling wind.

"Morag. You're safe and sound. These two have done well to find you," said Ian mor.

"Aye, but wait till we tell you the story, Ian. You'll not be believing it!" replied his brother.

They wrapped the unconscious man in a space blanket and made a birch stretcher. They trecked back along the shoreline. Sgian wondered if the Professor had suspected the water kelpie was a Viking longboat.

Heavy rain again. Sasha ran on ahead. She stopped and barked, the hair on her back bristling.

Sgian ran on, shouting, "What is it, Sasha?"

He saw a body. His heart sank. The black figure lay face down on a grassy promontory.

"Sasha's found a body!" he shouted.

He ran to the body. But the body had gone!

"It's an empty wet suit!" shouted Sgian.

"Looks like the other Norwegian's made a run for it," said the policeman.

The ambulance was waiting when they reached the road. The Norwegian recovered consciousness and when he reached the doctor's surgery he was able to tell his story.

"My colleague and I have been following Professor Sterne. She is suspected of being involved in the theft of an ancient gold piece. I went to search her hire boat while my colleague followed her car this morning. I remember opening a suitcase in the cabin. Then everything went blank. I awoke with a very painful head to find someone dressed in black putting a life jacket on me. The boat started rolling violently as if hit by a tidal wave. I was dragged up on deck and the last thing I remember was the boat capsizing."

Sgian didn't believe the Professor was a thief. Someone else was involved.

21

After supper, Mrs MacKenzie, her next-door neighbour and the boy sat in the kitchen, looking through horizontal rain towards a wild sea. The telephone rang.

"Hello, Jessie. It's Ian Cross. Has the Professor returned?"

"No, Ian. I'm very worried. She said she'd be back by tea time."

"The keeper at Dundonnel told me the road's flooded. She may have delayed her journey or turned back. I'll be round in the morning."

A few minutes later there was a knock at the door. Sasha barked. An elderly, bespectacled, grey-bearded man wearing a dripping cap adorned with fishing flies came in. He was stooped and carried a battered-looking brown leather bag.

"It's only me, Jessie," he said.

"Oh, it's yourself, Dr MacB. Come away in. Janice is here and this is Sgian," said Mrs MacKenzie.

"I'm glad to meet the wee hero," said the doctor.

When Sgian stood up from behind the kitchen table the doctor's eyes widened. He stared at the kilt. They shook hands and then he turned to Mrs MacKenzie, saying, "I just dropped in to see how you're managing."

"I'm being well looked after, Doctor. Will you take a cup of tea?" she said.

"I'm fine, Jessie. I'll wait till I get home and have something a bit stronger," he said with a smile. The two ladies chuckled.

"I wish MacKenzie would waken up, Doctor," said the old lady.

"It'll take time, Jessie. Since I started in medicine fifty years ago I've seen miracles happen with all the advances. He'll pull through. And

I can see you're in good hands. Don't hesitate to get in touch. I'd better go now and face the elements. I'll see myself out. Goodnight, everyone." He picked up his bag and left.

"He's a grand doctor, Jessie," said the other lady. "When he saw your kilt, Sgian, I think he was minded of one of the orphan boys he looked after. It was a terrible tragedy. The mother and one bairn went over a cliff. It was a miracle he was found alive on the beach among the seals. Her body was never found. He was a bright boy."

"Too bright, you might say. He was involved in some research scandal at St Andrews and wasn't allowed to take his medical degree," said Mrs MacKenzie.

"What became of him, Jessie?"

"I heard he went to America," she replied.

"His brother and stepbrother had a terrible accident at the fishing. I think it was a shark or something," said the lady.

The rain was torrential all night long. A worried-looking boy gazed out of the kitchen window at the white-topped waves. He was worrying about the Professor. Mrs MacKenzie phoned the police station to tell the constable that the Professor had not returned.

"And there's more bad news, Jessie. I've just heard from one of the fishermen that there's been a landslide at Gruinard Bay. A tourist bus and cars are involved. We'll need every available help. Could I pick up Sasha? She might be needed for searching. And Sgian could be her handler," the policeman said.

The old lady turned to relay the message to the boy.

"The Professor might be in one of the cars," said the boy.

Constable Cross, Sgian and Sasha arrived at the scene. Wind, rain, mist, rushing water and chaos. The steep road below them was blocked by a massive landslide. New rivers frothed and tumbled down the mountainside across the submerged road. Among the mass of mud, trees and boulders the tops of a bus and two cars were visible. Two men were clearing debris from the windows and doors of the vehicles. Another was tying a rope to one car hanging at an angle. It was on the verge of falling into the sea. Moving shapes were just visible through gaps in the mud-smeared windows of both vehicles. Two motorcyclists, looking like chocolate soldiers, were trying to scramble up the mud slope. Only the rear wheels of their machines were visible.

Sgian pointed to a car that was already in the water. The policeman took out his binoculars.

"That's the Professor's car. You two stay here. Watch for any further movement of the mud. Blow Sasha's whistle if you see any signs. I'm going down to join the others," said Ian Cross.

As the policeman descended through the debris, Sgian looked around for any moving mud.

"There's no mud up here, Sasha. Let's try and help the Prof. We'll go down," he said.

22

A deep throbbing sound. A Royal Navy helicopter appeared and landed on a section of disused single-track road overlooking the bay. The pilot, dressed in a bright orange flying suit, jumped down. He joined the rescue team.

"Jim Gibson from HMS *Falmouth*. I was on my way to drop a marker buoy for target practice when I spotted the landslide. Thought you might need some help with lifting," said the Lieutenant Commander.

"You're a Godsend, sir. Airsea rescue are already out on a call with the mountain rescue team. We can certainly use your help," replied Ian Cross.

A small bespectacled man in a yellow sou'wester, a green oilskin coat down to his ankles and white wellies joined them.

"Mercy me. It's yourself, Reverend MacLean," said the policeman.

"I've come to lend a hand. And you may have need of spiritual help," he said with a wink, patting a hip flask.

"And what's this story about the Stone of Destiny, Ian?" he added.

The policeman laughed. "You'll never believe it, Reverend, but Morag and MacKenzie knew where the real Stone was hidden in the loch and some character retrieved it only to be dragged into the loch by a Viking wreck."

They laughed.

"If anyone else had told me, I wouldn't believe it, Ian. Though I always thought we didn't know everything about Morag's involvement in that student escapade," said the minister.

"But that's not all. The lad from Edinburgh thinks the Viking boat is heading out to sea with the Stone underwater!" said the policeman.

There was a cough behind them. They turned.

"Ah, Dr Aboud. That's good of you to come and help." Ian Cross introduced him.

An olive-skinned man with a wide, flat nose, small dark eyes and short, black curly hair. He was dressed in full mountaineering gear.

"This gentleman's an experienced mountaineer. He's volunteered to help dig out survivors," said the policeman.

"Omar Aboud at your service. I've experience in abseiling. Perhaps I could assist in the helicopter," said the Egyptian.

"You're just the man we need, sir. Shall we get started?" said the pilot.

"Lead on!" said the Egyptian. As he walked towards the aircraft he sent a text: 'Prepare for island landing. Target location to follow.' Thanks to the boy he now had his plan B.

The helicopter worked hard, rescuing and ferrying the tour bus passengers to the village hall where Dr MacB and the district nurse dealt with casualties. The aircraft then returned to the landing site above Gruinard Bay. The Lt Commander and Aboud were given hot drinks.

"Well done, sir. I think that mission was a great success," said the pilot. He drained his mug of tea and then added, "Can I drop you off somewhere?"

"That is indeed kind. Anywhere near Poolewe will be convenient," he replied.

"If you climb aboard I'll inform the policeman," said the pilot.

The Egyptian climbed aboard. With the skill of a stage magician he grasped the thumb of his left hand and removed it. He shook the flesh-coloured artificial digit like a salt cellar and sprinkled a fine dust into the pilot's helmet, then replaced the thumb. The pilot returned, put his helmet on and strapped himself in. He smiled for a moment but then his face lost all expression. He gazed into the distance in a trance.

Aboud spoke in a low monotone. "I require your services. My command overrules any other authority. On a given signal you will drop the target buoy at a designated location. You will ensure that a missile is fired on that location. In a moment I shall count to three. You will awaken and have no recollection of these instructions but will carry them out when required. One, two, three."

The pilot blinked once or twice, smiled and then said, "Hold tight for lift off."

23

Sgian and Sasha climbed down the mud-covered slope onto the beach. He watched a fireman paddling a small inflatable boat towards the Professor's car. The water level was halfway up the windows. The driver's door was open. The fireman looked inside and shouted, "There's no one in the car. Her body must have been washed out to sea."

The boy's heart sank. He hugged Sasha. They stayed like that for a while, gazing out to sea. Eventually, he stood up, looked at the muddy slope and said, "Let's walk along the beach. I don't think there'll be any more mud slides."

Sasha ran on ahead towards some rocks. She stopped, sniffed, scratched between two seaweed-covered boulders, then took something in her mouth and ran back to the boy. She dropped a small, soggy, leather-bound notebook at the boy's feet.

"Good find, Sasha. That's what 'White Suit' dropped in the boat," he said. He sat down and opened the front cover. 'F. Bellamy. Astrodata' was written in pencil. An image flashed before his eyes. Like fast-forwarding a film. Two figures were roped together crossing a glacier. Suddenly, the one in front disappeared, the rope running fast into a crevasse. The one behind pushed his ice axe into the snow and stopped the other's descent. He pulled on the rope. A backpack appeared from the edge of the crevasse. The figure grasped the sack and cut the rope. The image was gone.

The other pages were all stuck in a soggy mass. He stood up.

"Must belong to that girl," he said, trying to understand what he had just seen.

They started to pick their way among the mud-splattered rocks back up the slope. There was a rumbling sound. Sasha barked. Sgian looked up.

"One giant cowpat heading our way, Sasha. Run!" he shouted.

The mud caught up with them. It brought his head down first. He pitched backwards, tumbling head over heels. Then he was was spinning through the air in the dark.

"Sasha!" he shouted. But she'd been left behind or sent tumbling on her own.

He was being squeezed. His head, arms, chest and legs felt waves of compression as if pummelled by giant fists. Grit and stone-filled earth battered him. The flying mud changed shape and consistency from moment to moment. Light flashed in and out of spaces between rocks and mud. A momentary glimpse of sky then sea.

'Disney World's got nothing on this,' he thought. Then he realised that he was lying on his skateboard gripping it tightly. He caught sight of a choppy, blue-green sea for an instant before plunging into the water. He shot back up to the surface and saw a large bird hovering high above. He heard the distant beat of a helicopter. There was growling, howling and yelping all round him. He felt heavy blows to his back and was squeezed between two slippery, moving bodies. A sharp pain shot through one arm followed by violent tugging on the sleeve of his jacket. One moment his head was above water, the next his mouth and nose were filled with the sea as waves crashed over him. His jacket collar was wrenched upwards and he was swinging in mid-air. Sgian felt hands take hold of his arms.

The Egyptian, scanning with binoculars from the open helicopter, saw the action and noted the submarine's course.

24

Sgian was lifted onto the casing of a submarine. A spotlight dazzled him from the conning tower. The boat was pitching and rolling.

A large man in a red sou'wester and waterproof shouted against the wind, "These bloodthirsty seals almost had a prize catch! They've taken a bit of your jacket and left teeth marks on your arm. Welcome aboard the *Rodt Foks*. Let's get you below and dried out, young man." A familiar voice greeted the boy as he climbed down a ladder into the warmth of the submarine's control room.

"I knew we'd meet again, Sgian," said the Professor.

"Me too, Anna," said the boy. They hugged.

She was dressed in a bright pink polo-necked jumper, black leather trousers and red leather boots.

"Warm submariner's clothes and a cup of hot soup coming up," said Lars. "Carl, our engineer, is built to crawl along small spaces. He's donated his ski pants and jumper," he added.

"You had a close call with some unfriendly creatures. I have a feeling they were on a mission," said the Professor.

Then the boy remembered Sasha.

"Where's Sasha? She must have been washed into the sea with me."

The Professor shouted something in Norwegian up the conning tower to one of the crew.

"We have a powerful searchlight. If she's nearby we'll find her. But these seals were really vicious."

They searched in vain.

"Let's hope she swam back to the shore. The mainland is close. Her survival instinct is strong," said the Professor.

As the boy took off his jacket the soggy notebook and a piece of rock fell out of his pocket.

"Your notebook looks in a sorry state. Can I dry it out for you?" asked the Professor.

"I think it belongs to the father of the girl who fell off her horse," said the boy.

"And where did you find this unusual rock? It's made of magnetite and limestone. I've never seen anything like it. You must show me," she said with great excitement.

"Keep it, if you like. I'll take you there." Then he told her about the Cave of Gold.

As the Professor placed the book on a radiator it opened. She saw a sketch of something that she immediately recognised.

"That looks like an Arctic island I was planning to visit," she said.

They drank hot soup in her cabin in silence, then the Professor recounted the day's events.

25

"**My** trip to Inverness didn't work out. Passing Loch Maree I saw a figure in black swim out to my boat. I went to investigate and found a man tied up in the cabin. He was a Norwegian detective. I managed to free him before the 2000-year-old Viking longboat capsized the launch. That was quite something."

"We saw that from the shore. That's what everyone thought was the kelpie, isn't it?" said the boy.

"And the Loch Ness monster, if my theory's correct. I hope the Norwegian's alright," she said.

Sgian nodded.

"I went back to my car and set off for Inverness, but someone was following me, so I doubled back and parked the car near Gruinard Bay. I used an inflatable to reach the sub. We heard about the landslide and my drowning on the radio."

"Why are the Norwegian police after you?" asked Sgian.

"I 'borrowed' a Viking object from the Oslo museum."

She opened a shoebox. It contained a flat, horn-shaped, translucent, reddish-gold object.

"It's a big gold sgian. Is that the thing on the carving?" said the boy.

"I think it is," she said, smiling.

"Can I hold it?"

She took it out of the box and handed it to him. He held it like a dirk and was fascinated by the way it glinted in the light.

"It's heavy, isn't it? What's it made of?"

"It's a mystery, Sgian. And you're right; it's heavier than the sort of rock it looks like," she said. "I was going to look up historical archives in the library. There's a story of sacred objects brought from Egypt to Isle Maree. An ancestor of mine was a Viking chief called The Red Fox. He visited this coast and was caught in some natural disaster. His boat sank. He was rescued and brought this object back to Norway. It was found in his burial chamber. It was thought to be quartz, but I noticed a faint image of the object was being etched on the glass case. That suggested it was a reactive material, so I gave a sample to a chemist colleague who has been unable to identify it. I think The Red Fox was caught up in an underwater earthquake triggered by a geochemical reaction."

Sgian remembered the story he'd heard from the Jacobite girl.

"We saw someone on your boat trying to lift something heavy out of the water. Was that the Stone that Morag hid?" asked the boy.

"Yes, and now it's in the longboat with the remains of my motor boat," she said.

"Morag told us the Stone broke in two and MacKenzie hid the other piece, but didn't know where," he said.

"We need to find both pieces to answer a very important question," said the Professor. "The sunken longboat is being carried by underwater currents along a fault in the earth's crust from Loch Ness to Loch Maree. Stories of monsters appearing in Loch Maree and Loch Ness from time to time are beginning to make sense. The intermittent appearance of the boat might depend on rainfall and earth tremors. It could well be heading out to sea along the same subterranean channel that sucked it down after the explosion long ago." She drew a line on her map that ran from Loch Maree to an island in the Atlantic Ocean. "I made a rough calculation of the speed of the current from watching that hat floating in the mine shaft. The longboat will soon be close to that island. Underwater forces around the island must reverse its course so it returns the way it came."

"You mean it just keeps going back and forwards?" asked the boy.

"And popping up from time to time where there are breaks in the channel," the Professor replied. She pointed at the map. "That's exactly what we're about to do, Sgian. We're heading for that island. I'm hoping the longboat will surface nearby."

"That's the island MacKenzie wanted to explore. It's called the Isle of Splashing Seals," said the boy.

"You've just joined our expedition. I hope you enjoy your first sleep in a submarine," said the Professor.

Sgian flopped back in a narrow bunk. A red glow, warm air smelling of diesel oil and continuous vibration sent him to sleep. He awoke with a change in sound and motion. The image of a dream lingered for a few seconds. He saw the Professor trapped in an iceberg.

26

Early morning. Grey mist. Grey Atlantic swell. The submarine conning tower.

"How do you know where you're going in this weather?" asked Sgian, straining to see.

"Radar for eyes and sonar for ears," said Lars, pointing to a screen. "That's the island we're heading for. It should be visible shortly."

The Professor climbed up to join them.

"The chart shows sheer cliffs all round. Like a vertical volcano," she said.

Minutes later a dark shape loomed up ahead.

"Have a look, Sgian."

Lars handed the boy a pair of binoculars. All three focussed on the shape. Massive black slabs of rock piled one on top of another formed a steep pyramid. The mist cleared to reveal a roughly flattened summit. Waves crashed against rocks all around its base.

"See anywhere to land?" asked the Professor.

"I don't even see birds," said the boy.

"Good observation. I wonder why?" she said.

"MacKenzie said only seals come here, and once he saw lights," said Sgian.

"Maybe your volcano's not so extinct, Anna," added Lars.

"Sonar shows gap in rock face," shouted one of the crew from below.

"Bottom depth?" enquired Lars.

"Thirty metres dropping to over 600, Lars," was the reply.

"Our volcano's sitting on a fault," said the Professor. "Let's do what the seals do. Prepare to dive," she added.

27

The *Rodt Foks* surfaced inside a lagoon open to a darkening sky. Clouds of grey-green mist drifted over still water, concealing its full extent.

"Phew! What a smell," said Sgian.

"There's sulphur in the air," said the Professor as they climbed up to the conning tower.

"Contact at 500 metres," said a voice from below.

"Slow ahead. We'll try to get out of this smog," said Lars.

Visibility improved. A huge silver dome emerged from the mist. It sat on a ledge overhanging a black sandy beach.

"What's that?" said the three observers almost in unison.

"Let's find out. Bring up the inflatable and life jackets, Lars," said the Professor.

A boat was lowered onto the dark water. The Professor jumped aboard first.

"I hope the kelpie's not lurking here somewhere," said the boy as he climbed down, clutching his skateboard.

Lars smiled.

"I like a lifeboat I can handle," said Sgian.

"Don't worry, Sgian, Lars is one of Norway's best shots," the Professor replied.

Lars joined them, a high-powered rifle with telescopic sight slung round his shoulder. He sat in the stern to work the outboard.

"Stay in contact on the surface, Nils," Lars said to the second mate.

They set off for the shore. They were almost halfway there when a blue flash lit up the lagoon. The fog vanished. A glimpse of black jagged cliffs with stunted trees growing out of crevices. A clap of thunder. More lightning. Below the volcanic opening a large overhanging rock. Sgian was terrified. They crouched low but continued to watch.

"What's that?" shouted the boy, pointing towards the cliff face opposite the overhang. With the next flash the Professor and Lars looked up. Something was moving on the rock face. It looked like a giant black bat.

The storm passed. A few wisps of blue flame flickered on the surface of the water, then died. All became silent.

The Professor spoke. "What do you think, Lars?"

"No idea, but I've a bad feeling," he replied.

"Ooo-hu. Ooo-hu. Ooo-hu. Oo-oo," an owl shrieked.

"Look at these bubbles," said Sgian.

A deep rumbling sound. Huge bubbles burst all around them. The boat started to spin. The engine was wrenched from its moorings. Lars hung on. He was whipped into the water without saying a word. The boat stood on end. The Professor and Sgian were thrown into the water. The boy clung on to the skateboard. The boat was sucked into a whirlpool. The lagoon was a spinning, raging sea. They were drawn to the vortex. Water filled Sgian's mouth and nose as his head was submerged. Something heavy bumped against his side, pushing him away from the whirlpool. He saw the Professor rising out of the water. Something dark brown and shiny carried her some way towards the shore. A large seal with a scar on its head rose up from the waves between them and the whirlpool. With powerful strokes of its massive flippers it created a wave that pushed them both out of danger to the shore.

They both reached the black beach coughing and retching. The seal watched them for a few moments then dived. The water calmed.

Standing on the beach they looked out over the still lagoon. No sign of Lars or the submarine. They remained silent for a few moments. Then the boy spoke.

"That seal with the scar on its head saved us, Anna. This may seem weird, but I recognised its eyes. They made me think of a classmate who drowned."

The Professor was nodding.

"It did seem to know what it was doing. I hope Lars was as lucky. He's one of Norway's Olympic swimmers. The two-way radio works underwater and the sub will have sent out a diver. Fingers crossed. Come on, Sgian, we'll investigate that dome."

The black volcanic sand seemed to swallow their feet as they walked up the beach. Behind the dome a series of steep ridges wound up towards the semicircular summit. They were composed of black rock slabs with trees and shrubs here and there. There was neither sound nor sight of birds.

"Look! Wires running up the cliffs," said Sgian.

"There must be a cable car. Let's find it. We've got to get out of here," said the Professor.

They discovered steps cut in the cliff face and climbed up behind the dome.

"There's the entrance and a landing platform. It must go to the summit," said the Professor.

The wires vibrated. They both looked up.

"It's coming down. Let's keep out of sight until we see who's on board."

They ran up the steps to a crevice from where the platform was visible. The cable car doors opened. A Jack Russell terrier jumped out barking. He was followed by a red-haired woman, a man in a white suit and a monk. The woman was speaking.

"...The fire put an end to my modelling career so I went to medical school."

"Your colleague thinks highly of you, Dr Kirk. But is this really the best place for your skills?"

She touched her scarred face and said, "For the moment."

'White Suit' looked at his watch. "My transport arrives in thirty minutes. Will the helo pad be clear?"

The redhead nodded.

"Would you like to inspect your lichen? The brethren tell me they can see it grow and it seems to be consuming everything in its path," said the monk.

'White Suit' looked surprised and said, "That I must see. Go on ahead. We shall follow presently."

The monk started up the steps followed by the terrier. As the woman was about to follow, 'White Suit' grasped his left thumb and held his right hand close to her face. After a few seconds all expression disappeared from her face. The man spoke to her slowly.

"Will Nochd keep his promise?"

She shook her head. He murmured something. She turned and, like a sleepwalker, went down the steps towards the dome. 'White Suit' walked up the steps.

"What d'you make of that, Sgian?" asked the Professor.

"I think she's been drugged," he replied.

"We've got to get out of here. They must have come by helicopter. Let's go up. See if I can remember how to fly a chopper," she said, smiling.

28

An ear-splitting screech echoed around the rocky cliffs. They were both knocked to the ground and enveloped in darkness. Sharp talons pierced their clothes. They lay pinned to the ground under foul-smelling cloaks. The covering was removed. In dim light they saw a ghastly sight. Standing over them were two deformed men. Each had a blue scar on one side of the head. No eyebrows or lashes. Eyes bloodshot. Hooked noses with flared, crusted nostrils. Lips thin, red and drawn back in a fixed grimace. One held the limp, half-chewed body of a rat between black teeth. Each man had a smoking canister slung round his neck.

The Jack Russell barked. The monks jumped back against the rock wall. The terrier appeared, followed by the two men they had seen earlier.

"It's the boy from the beach. And, if I'm not mistaken, Professor Sterne," said 'White Suit'. "My name is Aboud, and you know the whereabouts of the gold horn and the longboat, Professor."

She said nothing.

"Let me jog your memory. I have a rather special plant to show you," said Aboud.

The Professor and Sgian were taken up steps to the overhang opposite a rock face. Aboud pointed across a ravine.

"Watch!"

He snatched the half-chewed rat from the birdman's mouth and threw it towards the rock, still in shadow. The Jack Russell, true to its instinct, leapt into the void after the furry bundle. There was no sound.

Both bodies stuck to the lichen like flies on flypaper.

A break in the clouds. A watery sun shone into the island crater. A sheet of black lichen rippled, visibly expanding over the wet rock face. The tail and hind legs of the dog protruded from the moving growth. Directly below but separated by a gap of about ten metres was a steep, grassy slope. It fell away into the dark depths of the ravine. The grass was topped by a thick bed of heather.

Aboud nodded to the two birdmen. Sgian was pulled to the edge of the overhang. He was terrified.

"Answer my question or watch your young friend fly," said Aboud.

Without hesitation the Professor shouted, "The longboat should appear near longitude 6, latitude 58."

"And the gold horn?" the man asked.

The Professor hesitated. It was in the submarine. 'Have they managed to escape from the whirlpool? Has Lars been rescued? We Vikings are survivors. I will not endanger my crew,' she thought.

The skateboard was waiting and ready to go. It faced the abyss. Images flashed through the boy's mind.

He'd jumped two metres before, but this was something else. And where would the slope end? It looked almost vertical. He recalled seeing a film about a man free-riding a snowboard down Mount Everest. But that had been his last ride! No time for second thoughts, even in daylight!

"Here goes, Prof!" he shouted.

The shout and its echoes took everyone by surprise. He twisted round, freeing himself from his captors, grabbed the Professor's arm and pulled her onto the back of his skateboard.

Aboud stretched out an arm and caught Sgian by the hair. The boy dug his nails into the hand. The man screamed and withdrew the hand minus a 'thumb'. Sgian launched the board into mid-air.

"What? Oh no...!" the Professor yelled. The breath was taken from her.

Someone else had quick reactions and swooped after them. But a monk's habit doesn't have the aerodynamics of a skateboard. The man who'd been made to think he was an owl plummeted into darkness. His screech echoed all the way down. A real eagle owl took off and swooped after them.

Sgian and the Professor landed still upright in the spongy heather bed across the gap. Thick heather is like a springboard. They bounced down the slope into the gloom. Sgian's night vision was like that of a wildcat.

The board rushed faster and faster, the owl in pursuit.

Sgian felt the Professor's grip tighten on his shoulders each time they zigzagged around rocks. They jumped a waterfall. The skateboard spun through 360 degrees after glancing off a rockface. Sgian's muscles were tense, anticipating each manoeuvre.

Leathery wings flapped in his face as they crashed through a flock of bats. Sgian looked round. He recognised the eagle owl with its mobile phone. It turned away, two bats in its talons and one in its beak.

'A bat in the beak's worth more than two on a skateboard,' he thought.

A patch of light showed up ahead. The next moment they were in the open. Thump, shudder, squelch. Board, boy and Professor came to a sudden stop and were thrown head first into a peat bog. After spluttering, shaking their heads and wiping mud from their eyes they laughed at each other's appearance.

Standing on shaky legs, they saw the lagoon a short way below. Sgian opened his hand. It had been clenched tightly since he'd snatched Aboud's 'thumb' containing the drug. He handed it to the Professor.

"Might come in handy, Sgian," she said, putting it in her pocket.

"It's stuffy down here," said the boy.

"You're right, Sgian. And have you noticed the bubbles all over the lagoon? I think it's methane. This place is a ticking time bomb. We've got to get out fast."

They walked around a headland. The dome towered over a boathouse set into the rockface. A motorboat was tied up inside. A fishing boat was moored close to a slipway nearby.

"That boat must have just arrived," said the Professor.

"It's the *Highland Warrior*. My father's her skipper," said the boy.

"If it got in, we're going out the same way," said the Professor, pointing to the far end of the lagoon. "It's low tide. There's an entrance above water now. Let's go aboard."

They went down to the beach and walked to the slipway.

"Anyone about?" shouted the Professor.

There was no reply. They walked up a gangplank and climbed steps up to the bridge. The Professor saw binoculars and a chart lying beside the satnav screen. Sgian went in to the skipper's cabin and put his skateboard under the bunk. He caught sight of something familiar.

"I'll have a closer look at the entrance," said the Professor, picking up the binoculars.

A voice that seemed familiar to Sgian boomed out from a cabin,

"Welcome. Fortune favours those who wait."

A large man appeared at one end of the bridge. Then a familiar figure stepped out of the cabin, the eagle owl on his shoulder. For a few seconds Sgian recognised the American. The man put one hand behind his head and pulled. His bald head, dark eyebrows, bulbous nose and black moustache were peeled off. The ruddy complexion was replaced by a pale, wrinkled, pockmarked face. His lips were thin and scarred. There were no eyebrows or lashes. His nose was like an eagle's beak covered in stretched, thin skin. His head looked like a shrubbery. Clumps of grey hair sprouted on a pale, scarred scalp. There was a surgical dressing on one side of his head.

"My name is Nochd Maree, alias Oliver Jeffrey the second. You see before you the results of my early attempts to tame a carnivorous lichen." He tried to smile. The result was a twisting of his upper lip to reveal a yellow canine tooth. "This is my brother. And you, Sgian Maree Dubh, are a distant relative. Eoin has kept me informed of your whereabouts." He stroked the bird. "Judging from the peat stains, you've been exploring my island. Perhaps you saw the magnificent lichen that will be hailed as the 21st century's wonder drug? Now you'll see the jewel in the crown when I explore the boy's brain. You, Professor Sterne, will tell my brother the whereabouts of the Stone. And later I have another use for the Professor's cerebral matter in mind."

29

ochd's tight grip around Sgian's arm forced him towards the dome. But a remarkable change had come over the boy. His leap into space in daylight had produced a feeling of calm. Yet his senses were finely tuned. He felt no fear.

They approached the main door.

"My operating theatre is designed for hyperbaric surgery. Your ears will pop when we enter," said Nochd.

They passed through an airlock into a brightly lit, tiled operating theatre. With one beat of its wings, the owl reached a perch. It bent its head to start recording the proceedings.

A maze of equipment and monitors surrounded two complicated-looking operating couches in the middle of the space. At the head end of each couch was a gantry carrying a helmet with multiple attachments. Surgical instruments were laid out under transparent plastic covers on trolleys.

The red-haired woman, dressed in surgical clothes, entered from another door. Sgian thought she still looked dazed. He was lifted into one of the chairs. He saw himself in a large, illuminated magnifying mirror overhead.

His 'host' became Donald Duck and the red-haired woman became Jemima Puddleduck as they conversed in high-pitched voices, an effect of breathing an oxy-helium mixture to prevent the 'bends'. Sgian smiled. He would not be made to speak.

"Prepare him for craniotomy and give the muscle relaxant," said Donald Duck.

He climbed onto a couch, removed the dressing from his head and put on a helmet. A mask was placed over Sgian's nose and mouth. He was aware of a sweet smell. His limbs felt heavy. They wouldn't move. His head was shaved.

Donald Duck spoke. "I have been pursuing your brain for over a decade. I thought your mother's brain cells might have the second sight. But my equipment failed. I now have the perfect instrument and the perfect immunosuppressant lichen with which to make medical history."

A helmet was placed on Sgian's head. Nochd removed something like an electric plug from his head. Sgian was transfixed by Nochd's sinister gaze as he quacked a description of the procedure.

"The Magnetron will stimulate your brain and transmit the image to my brain. I will locate and extract the second sight neurones, treat with lichen, then transplant them into my brain."

The Magnetron made a deep humming sound. He saw zigzag lines, flashing lights, places and faces in quick succession. Sounds of jumbled voices, howling wind and weird music. A musty, burning smell…

A clear image came into his mind. He was looking at a woman running up a hill pursued by a figure in a cloak. She was breathing hard. Struggling with every step. Her pursuer shouted, "You can't escape, Mairi Maree. If you won't tell me where the boy is I will take something from you."

Sgian heard her say, " Burn the Stone to banish the dark."

Then the image was gone.

High-pitched, excited quacking from the other couch: "I've found the second sight! Amazing! He has an exact memory of an event that he never witnessed. Prepare for the transplant, Gail."

There was no reply from the woman. Sgian heard a hissing sound.

"Gail, take my helmet off! Arm the Neurodissector," shouted Donald Duck. But the woman had gone.

"A hole in my head and brain suction. No way!" Sgian said to himself. He tried to move. Nothing happened. But his brain was alert. In fact he'd never felt more alert. Ever since that flight on the skateboard… and no fear of the height. In daylight!

Donald Duck started to rise from his chair.

'There must be a way out. If only I could paralyse him,' thought the boy. Then Sgian remembered the American's words on the train: "High places don't agree with me." Fear can paralyse. Sgian closed his eyes and relived jumping off the ledge on the skateboard. He felt himself falling. Faster and faster. The board was flying. He was in control and enjoying it.

But Donald Duck wasn't. He was screaming in terror as vivid images flashed before him and brought back the horror of his fall as an infant.

The hissing sound was louder. Sgian felt he was being compressed. His ears were painful. Donald Duck stopped screaming, became silent and motionless. Sgian's arms and legs began to work again. He rolled off the couch and landed on his face and chest. He couldn't focus. He turned onto his back. The light became red. He blacked out.

30

Ronachan pushed the Professor into the skipper's cabin and sat her down.

"Tell me about these relics. The Stone I almost took from the loch was broken. Where's the other piece and the gold Aboud talks about?" he croaked, straining his damaged vocal cords.

She looked around the cabin for a weapon. A red suitcase and large Holy Bible lay on a table.

"Bring me the chart from the bridge," she said.

He stepped out. She stood up. The moment he returned, she thrust the drugged 'thumb' under his nose. He sneezed, half raised his arms and stood absolutely still with a glazed look in his eyes. She lifted up the Holy Bible, climbed onto the chair and brought the heavy tome down with a thump on his head.

"Blessings be upon you!" she said.

The man fell down.

"Now, where's Sgian's father," she said, running onto the bridge.

She found him tied up in the hold. While releasing him she outlined the situation.

"I know where Sgian is and I have an effective weapon," she said, holding up the drugged 'thumb'. "Can you drag the big man onto the beach and prepare to sail?"

Sgian's father nodded in agreement, though not quite understanding anything.

"Time is short," he said. "The tide's turning. And another thing; we must rescue my crew. They're locked up on Gruinard Island."

The redhead, still in a hypnotic trance, closed the airlock and turned up the pressure in the theatre. She took the cable car up to the helo pad. Four men in wetsuits were checking lifting gear on a large helicopter. Aboud was talking by mobile to the hypnotised Naval officer.

"Launch the missile in 30 minutes on target long. 6, lat. 58." He terminated the call as the redhead appeared.

"Ah, Gail! Task completed?"

She nodded.

"Come and meet my team. The best mercenary divers money can buy. You will join us to watch the recovery of the Sacred Stone when the longboat is blown to the surface. Then we shall rescue the gold horn from the Professor's submarine. I am certain that is where we shall find it. Time to go."

The Professor ran up the beach to the dome. She glanced through an observation window. Sgian lay motionless on the floor of the operating theatre. Nochd's body was convulsing, eyes staring in terror, mouth frothing.

She switched off the compressor, grabbed oxy-helium breathing gear and burst through the door. Out of the corner of her eye she saw a shadow move rapidly across the wall of the dome. She was knocked to her knees and enveloped in a heavy blanket of twitching feathers. She screamed. The unconscious owl fell from her shoulders.

She pushed the mask onto Sgian's face, lifted him onto her shoulders and ran out. By the time they reached the boat he was awake. His father helped them up to the cabin. No words passed between father and son.

The *Highland Warrior*, at full speed, crossed the lagoon and surged through the rapidly diminishing entrance, leaving her mast and radar antennae behind.

31

Sgian would remember the events of the next hour as if they were played out in slow motion. He had fully recovered. His voice sounded normal and the Professor declared him free from the 'bends'.

The fishing boat charged full ahead over a calm sea. Sgian and the Professor looked through the swirling bow waves. Each had a firm grip on the bridge rail.

"That villain Aboud and his men will be after us. Keep a lookout astern," said the Professor.

"So, where to?" asked Roderick Dubh.

The Professor went into the skipper's cabin and returned with a chart. Indicating a course with her finger, she said, "We must rendezvous with a Viking longboat somewhere along this track. Only two problems, however. They know the co-ordinates and it only remains on the surface for a few minutes." She smiled. "Let's hope Lady Luck's on our side!"

The skipper was shaking his head, not believing what he had just heard.

"A Viking boat? Surfacing? What are you talking about?"

"It's a family thing for the Prof," said his son.

Roderick's eyes widened further, if that were possible, but he said nothing.

"Look!" shouted the boy.

A bright orange object was bobbing in the sea ahead.

"A Navy target buoy. We'd better give it a wide..." The skipper's words were drowned out.

Whoosh! A missile ripped through the air no more than ten metres above the boat. It plunged into the sea close to the buoy. Sgian ducked without thinking and he could feel the hair stand up on the back of his neck. The Professor's knuckles whitened as she glanced over her shoulder.

"That was too close! Time to be elsewhere," shouted Sgian's father, pulling the wheel hard to port.

"No sign of any vessel behind," said the Professor.

"Probably long range practice," the man replied.

A moment later the sea under the boat rose up several metres. A deep rumble and vibration beneath their feet. A mountain of water erupted ahead of them. Huge bubbles erupted on the surface. A wide channel of foaming, swirling water rushed by them at a rate faster than any craft. They looked back to see it heading for the Isle of Splashing Seals. The Viking longboat burst to the surface in the midst of the boiling sea.

"That missile's triggered an earthquake in the fault!" shouted the Professor.

"The Stone!" shouted Sgian, pointing to a weed-covered object lying on the deck amid wreckage of the motor launch.

"Yes! But can we take it?" the Professor replied while taking photos of her ancestor's boat.

"What do you want that for?" asked the boy's father.

"It's the Stone of Destiny," shouted Sgian.

The man shook his head in disbelief and said, "Prof, take the wheel. Sgian, come with me. You work the winch. I'll cast the net and push the Stone in."

Man and boy flew down the ladder. Feet never touched one step. He showed Sgian the controls, cut open the 'cod end' of the net, hung on to it and shouted, "Cast off!"

The Professor's seamanship kept the vessels close together. She didn't hear the high-speed launch approaching nor see the figure jump aboard the *Highland Warrior*. Ronachan bounded up the steps to the bridge, shouted something in Gaelic, then slammed her against the skipper's cabin door. It burst open. She crashed into the chart table, knocking a red suitcase onto the floor. A serious-looking instrument fell out. She picked it up, charged back onto the bridge and switched it on. The neurodissector whined. Ronachan was at the wheel. He turned towards her.

Below on deck, Sgian watched his father swing over the longboat's deck, clinging to the net. He jumped onto its rolling, rotting deck beside the Stone. He pushed it into the net. His face was strained with the effort and his hands bleeding. He jumped on to the longboat's gunwale. The Viking ship was sinking fast.

A terrifying roar, which Sgian recognised, came from between the two vessels. The giant seal's wide-open jaws appeared. The lethal mouth clamped onto Roderick's head. His last words, "Raise the net!" were followed by a crunch of bone and a stomach-churning sucking sound as Roderick Dubh's brain was drawn into the seal's mouth.

Ronachan grabbed the drill, leapt from the bridge and plunged it into the beast's head.

"Basaich! Go back to Hell. Eoghain and I are avenged!"

The beast's huge flippers grasped its attacker. Three writhing bodies disappeared into the sea. The net containing the Stone swung back over to the fishing boat.

The sky darkened. A sudden gust of wind. A deep rumble louder than any thunder Sgian had ever heard. The sea rose up in giant, grey-green waves. Both Sgian and the Professor saw it at the same time, but the boy saw something else: a small red laser dot on the Professor's forehead.

The helicopter was less than 1000 yards away and closing fast on the *Highland Warrior*. The sniper was focussed. He'd been instructed to target the woman and awaited the command to squeeze the trigger. The videophone in Omar Aboud's hand was transmitting the image of the two figures on the fishing boat's bridge 1500 miles to Switzerland.

"The Sacred Stone is in that net suspended over the boat deck. Now you can enjoy watching an execution, Montez," Aboud shouted into the phone above the din of the helicopter's engine. But neither Aboud, his son nor the mercenaries on board saw the rapidly expanding black, slimy lichen mass that crept towards the main rotor.

"Look!" Sgian shouted up to the Professor, pointing to the helicopter. "That black slime's attacking the helicopter."

The engine spluttered. The flying machine wobbled. Four pairs of eyes turned to look at the pilot. He was struggling to control his machine. Then, every helicopter pilot's nightmare became reality. Silence.

Sgian and the Professor witnessed the somersault and final plunge of the aircraft into the sea. The *Highland Warrior* with the small launch tied alongside was alone on a calm sea. The Professor ran down the steps and put one arm around the boy's shoulders. No words were spoken for a while. Then he said, "I wish I'd known him better."

"You've inherited his spirit, Sgian. He'll be watching over you."

He nodded, took a deep breath and looked at the Stone in the net.

"What now?" he asked.

"Let's see if Lady Luck's still with us. I'll try to contact the *Rodt Foks*."

They both cheered when a familiar voice replied. The sub, her crew and Lars were alive and well. They arranged to rendezvous off the Laide beach.

"Let's build the Stone and the gold sgian into the walls of the ruined chapel. We'll need Lars to help us. I don't know how these students had the strength."

"We'll meet again then, Prof?" asked the boy.

"We're a team, remember, Sgian. I'll write and come over when MacKenzie tells you where the other part of the Stone is hidden," she replied.

Part of him wanted to go with her.

32

They reached the waters off Laide beach. The mini sub was waiting. Lars and Carl appeared on the conning tower, then transferred to the *Highland Warrior*.

"We'll tell the coastguard the fishing boat's here and the crew are on Gruinard Island," said the Professor.

"Here's your kilt, jacket and dried-out notebook, Sgian. Keep the stuff you're wearing. And here's a Lapp woolly hat," said Carl.

"Magic!" said Sgian, grinning.

Sgian went to retrieve his skateboard and something very special from the skipper's cabin. His father's faded green Royal Marine Arctic sleeping bag lay in one corner. It must carry many stories. This would be his inheritance. As he rolled it up an image came into his mind. He saw the Professor frozen inside an iceberg. A shiver ran down his spine.

He joined the others and the Stone in a dinghy. They landed on the beach below the ruined chapel. Lars and Carl carried the Stone together. The Professor had the gold sgian in the shoebox under her arm.

The Stone was positioned in a gap in the wall. The Professor compared the gold sgian's surface with the broken edge of the Stone. She turned it round and held it close to the Stone. There was a sharp crack. A sudden force pulled it to the irregular depression on the surface of the Stone. It was a perfect fit.

"Ow! What's happening? I'm tingling all over. I can't let go," she shouted.

"You're earthing a current, Anna. Jump on the boot!" said Lars, pulling off one of his long rubber seaboots and hurling it at her feet.

With some effort she lifted her feet onto the boot and was able to let go. She looked at her shaking hand.

"Look at that!"

There was a sparkling gold impression of the sgian handle on her palm. Despite rubbing, the mark remained.

"I've been tattooed. That was a powerful electromagnetic force. I'm no physicist, but I think this stuff is extraterrestrial. There may be a sort of critical mass thing going on here. The other half of the Stone will have a depression that is an exact fit for the sgian. Bring the three pieces together, throw in a touch of lightning and boom! You've got an earthquake or volcanic eruption. Sgian, you've got to find the other piece when MacKenzie awakes. I'll get a physicist involved and ask a sculptor friend of mine to make a copy of the sgian in carnelian for the museum. They'll be none the wiser. Just as Morag and her fellow students did with the Stone of Destiny."

"D'you think Aboud knew about this?" asked the boy.

"I think he did, Sgian. Maybe that gummed-up notebook's involved," she said.

While Lars, Carl and Sgian concealed the Stone and attached the sgian, Anna wrote a letter. She approached Sgian and gave him a big hug.

"Time for us to go and for you to get back to the MacKenzie house, Sgian. Give this letter to Jessie. She'll show it to the policeman. It gives a simplified account, so they won't need to ask you any questions. These were days I'll never forget, Sgian. Thank you. And take our map of the area. I've written comments on our routes all over it," said Anna. There were tears in her eyes. His tears were hidden in a hug.

"These were great times, Anna, and this is the best present ever. You solved your puzzle. I discovered a bit about my ancestors. But I learned a lot more from you. I'll be ready for our next expedition!"

"And that's soon. I know you'll find your way back to Jessie's. You're a star route finder, Sgian."

He shook hands with Lars and Carl then waved them off. As the three Norwegians climbed aboard the inflatable, Sgian shouted, "Stay away from icebergs, Anna."

She looked puzzled, smiled, then shouted back, "How did you know?"

He watched the submarine set course for the north. A light breeze. Heavy dark clouds. The tops of the mountains were hidden in mist. The only sounds were the waves breaking on the shore as he walked up the beach. Not a soul in sight.

He was about to set off on his board along the coastal road when it hit him. An empty feeling that comes with loss. His mother. His kitten. His father. Now Anna. He was alone.

"Morag was right. I am the last one. What is there to do? I've had enough of school. The Head can do his own stupid tasks. I'll tell Liz about Dad. She's going to be alright. It's time for me to…" He sat down on his skateboard and sobbed. After several minutes he looked up and wiped his eyes.

"Woof, woof!" Sasha was bounding towards him. Tail wagging furiously, tongue at the ready to welcome him back. They hugged and went home. It was raining.

An emotional Mrs MacKenzie was standing at the door. She read the letter.

"Someone's looking after you, Sgian. We all thought you'd been drowned. The coast guard's still searching, so I'll phone Ian to tell him the good news."

As he crawled into bed that night he heard a distant rumble of thunder.

33

Something was wrong. He was wide awake yet it was still dark. He jumped out of bed and looked out of the window. A thick, black cloud hung low over the sea. Headlights drew up and a black-faced policeman stepped out of his car. Sgian dressed and went downstairs to meet the delicious smell of frying bacon and a dust-covered Ian Cross.

"We've no idea where the dust cloud's come from. Never seen anything like it. Come to think of it, I've never known a week like it!"

"Could it no be someone burning heather, Ian?" suggested Mrs MacKenzie.

"No one's reported any fires, Jessie," the man replied. "I think it'll soon blow away. There's a bit of a breeze starting up. I just came round to say I'm going to Inverness this morning. So we can all go to see you off at the station, Sgian."

The policeman left and his prediction was correct. By the time the boy had finished breakfast the black cloud had gone.

"You've plenty time for a walk with Sasha before Ian comes round with his car," said Mrs MacKenzie.

They ran along the beach. Sasha chasing sea gulls, Sgian chasing thoughts. He stopped to look out to sea and thought of those he was leaving behind. Then it struck him. Something was different. The Isle of Splashing Seals had disappeared!

"The ticking time bomb's gone off!" he said out loud.

He called Sasha and as he turned to walk back to the village he saw a seal's head appear on the surface. It bared its teeth then dived.

There was something he didn't see. A piece of old timber was being washed ashore on Gruinard Island. It was covered in a black slime.

34

$\mathfrak{H}$is head shaven, a black eye, sticking plasters on both knees and a piece of his jacket sleeve missing, Sgian stood in the carriage doorway. He said goodbye to Mrs MacKenzie, Sasha and Constable Ian Cross. The boy was fighting back tears. The old lady's eyes were wet. Sasha's eyes said she wanted to come with him.

"Write soon, Sgian," said Mrs MacKenzie.

"And this lass here needs you on the hill!" said the policeman, giving Sasha a rub on the back of her neck.

"I'll be back," said Sgian.

A guard closed the door. A whistle was blown and the boy waved as the train departed.

The carriage was packed. People were standing in the passageway. A girl with hazel-coloured eyes and nut-brown hair was sitting reading a book in the seat close to the doorway. Two suntanned, middle-aged men had the window seats. They were studying a map of Edinburgh. Their arms were covered in midgie bites.

Sgian sat down opposite the girl. "Hi! Great to see you again."

She looked up and smiled. "It's you! I wondered when we'd meet again. That's a bit extreme! What happened?" she said, pointing to his head, black eye and battered knees.

"Climbing and things. A long story. How's the arm?" he said, lifting her bag and his skateboard up to the rack. He pushed his sack under the seat and sat down.

"Fine. Nothing broken, thanks to you. My daddy loved climbing," she said.

He caught the sadness in her eyes.

"What's wrong?"

"He was killed in the Alps," she said.

They looked at each other for a few moments. An image of two figures struggling on a glacier flashed through his mind. He would ask her about it later.

"I've been through it, too. My dad was drowned at sea," he said in a quiet voice.

She reached across the table and touched his hand. No words for a few more moments. Then she spoke. "The kilt's not made for climbing. How about tartan climbing breeches?"

He smiled. "What d'you mean?"

"My mum loves doing alterations."

Sgian was impulsive. He took the ski pants from his sack, pulled them on and removed the kilt.

"It's all yours. Just fresh from the wash."

She laughed. So did the two men sitting beside them.

"Well, that's a first. I hope you wouldn't do that for any girl," said Fiona.

"That's the only kilt I've got," he said, smiling. "What's the book?"

"It's one of my dad's astronomy books," she replied.

He remembered the notebook and bent down to take it from his sack. The train stopped at a small station.

"I'll take this to Mum," she said, leaving her seat.

"Hi, you two," Fiona said to a young fair-haired boy and a woman with a smiling face, brown eyes and greying black hair. Sgian was a few steps behind and caught a glimpse of a tiny bald patch on the side of the woman's head.

"This trip's just fine to finish this sock, Fi," she said.

"I've a special request, Mum." She held up the kilt.

The woman dropped her knitting. Her eyes widened. She reached for the tartan and said, "Tha Sgian feile beag."

Fiona had never heard her mother speak Gaelic. Then another Gaelic word from behind.

"Mathair."

In a blink Fiona understood. Harriet stood up. Sgian stepped into her arms. They hugged for a full minute and words of joy were smothered.

"It's my boy. It's Sgian," she said, tears running down her cheeks, much to the amazement of a smiling Fiona and her confused young brother.

"Mother left when you were a baby, Mike. Harriet's always been 'Mum' for us. Now we've a stepbrother!" Fiona said to her brother.

His eyes widened.

The train started to move. Sgian's mother, holding her son's hands and smiling, spoke.

"It's like awakening from a deep sleep. You'll have to help, Sgian. You'll come home with us, won't you?"

He nodded.

They returned to their seats. Fiona looked happy.

Sgian said quietly, "Tell me I'm not dreaming."

"It's for real, stepbrother! Mum recognised you instantly. I never knew she could speak Gaelic. She'd lost her memory after a head injury before Daddy met her."

"You called her Harriet. That was my auntie's name. She died when I was little. Mum's name's Mairi," he said.

"Were they twins?" asked Fiona.

"Yes," he said.

"That explains it. Apparently, the only identification found on your mum was a photo with the name 'Harriet' scribbled on the back."

"What about your real mother?" he asked.

"She left when I was five. Never seen her since. Your mum came along and made us all happy."

Sgian still had the notebook in his hands. He gave it to her.

"Dad's notebook! That's two miracles!" She took it with one hand and squeezed his hand with the other.

During the remainder of the journey Fiona was enthralled by Sgian's story. When he'd finished she said, "So, Aboud's gone. I wonder what his son in Switzerland will do? And what was that black stuff, Sgian?"

"No idea. I hope it all went to the bottom of the sea. But I don't think the story's over. I'm going to need your help, Fi," he said.

Edinburgh Waverley Station

"You three wait in the taxi queue. I'm going to get a postcard to send to Zurich," said Mairi.

Fiona nudged Sgian. He took his mother's hand and said, "He won't be coming back."

She looked into her son's eyes, understood his meaning and nodded slowly.

Fiona turned to a confused-looking Mike and said, "You know what, Mike? Life just got a lot more interesting!"

35

$\mathfrak{S}$ome weeks later there was a story in the *Edinburgh Evening News*: 'Missing schoolboy found wandering along beach. James Watt, a pupil at the Edinburgh School, who went missing while surfing, was found on Gullane beach. He had suffered a head injury and memory loss.'

Mairi, Fiona, Mike and Sgian were awaiting Mrs MacKenzie and Sasha when they arrived at Waverley station. Sgian got a special welcome from Sasha. He looked at her injured ear.

"It's healed fine," said Mrs MacKenzie.

As they sat in the taxi on the way to the Royal Infirmary the old lady said, "The hospital phoned me yesterday to say that MacKenzie was showing encouraging signs."

At the hospital entrance a porter offered to look after Sasha.

"Neurosurgery, fourth floor," said Sgian, pointing to a sign in the main concourse.

They approached the nurse's station and asked to be allowed to visit.

"He'll be delighted to see you," said the nurse, smiling.

"You mean he's wakened up?" said Mrs MacKenzie. All eyes brightened.

"It happened during the night. We're all amazed. He's in a single room. He has the best view in the hospital. Wash your hands before you go in."

As they walked in, MacKenzie, with a bandaged head, was gazing towards the River Forth. He turned and grinned from ear to ear. After hugs and handshaking, Sgian introduced Fiona, her brother and Mairi, promising to tell the full story later.

"A porter's waiting downstairs with Sasha. The nurse says we can take you in a wheelchair to see her," said Mrs MacKenzie. "And I've brought something for you."

She pulled his yellow and black tartan deerstalker hat from her bag and put it on top of his bandages. Everyone laughed. Sgian was aware of a faint smell just for a second or two.

"Now I know I'm on the road to recovery," said MacKenzie. "It's grand to be back in the land of the living and to see you all. Pity I can't see the Botanic Garden from here. But there's a blank in my memory. I can't remember going back home."

They would soon learn that he'd lost most of his long-term memory.

With tears of joy Mrs MacKenzie said, "There's plenty time for you to catch up. Just get your strength back so's they'll let you come home."

"Everything alright?" asked the nurse, looking round the door.

"It's nothing short of a miracle," said Mrs MacKenzie. "I'd like to thank the doctor."

"I'm afraid that won't be possible, Mrs MacKenzie. He was a visiting specialist from America."

"What was his name?" asked Sgian.

"Jeffrey, Mr Oliver Jeffrey," replied the nurse.

Fiona shot a puzzled look towards Sgian. His heart sank. Nochd had survived! Where and when would he reappear? Why had he come to operate on MacKenzie and save his life?

Sgian and Fiona were ahead of the others as they approached the automatic main door. It opened and a grey form leapt towards Sgian. The little cat he'd saved from drowning was in his arms, purring and rubbing its head against his chest.

"You've got a real friend there, brother," said a smiling Fiona.

"I forgot to tell you this part of the story. Meet Purdie," he said.

They walked a few steps then he stopped suddenly.

"I know why Nochd came back. He was exploring MacKenzie's brain for the hiding place of half of the Stone of Destiny!"